Jessie's Way

Joy Hilsman Thomas

ISBN #13:978-1540588647

ISBN #10:1540588645

Published 2016

Author's Note

"Here's looking at you, kid."

Humphrey Bogart, as Rick Blaine

Casablanca -- 1942

On August 25, 1942, during a black out in Atlanta, Georgia, a black-haired girl arrived in this world.

"Jessie's Way" is a short book of short stories, conveyed in the voice of that young girl. From the mid to late 1940s to the early to mid-1950s, truth is divulged in fiction.

Life within these stories tattles on itself in numerous and assorted ways, but who's to know the difference?

It is for this reason the reader must pick apart the truth.

Enjoy.

Joy

Buggerbears

"Ain't no Buggerbears out tonight,

Daddy done killed 'em all last night."

On a chilly Georgia night in March, as I was just

finishing third grade, our house burned to the ground. Other than the clothes on our bodies and my brother's old bicycle, we lost everything we owned.

It was the sort of night where a light sweater is perfect, but not wool because wool itches in the spring. Darcy was eleven and Bobby about five; I don't remember how old Mama and Daddy were. I do know it was on a Sunday night because the people who stopped to watch were on their way home after church. They couldn't do a thing to help because they had on their church clothes. They just had to watch it burn.

We had gone to our Uncle Sam's house after supper. Daddy needed to talk to his older brother about the cows he'd rented from Sam to get a start in the dairy business. It wasn't until later that word got out about Mama fussing at Daddy for putting pennies in the fuse box. She said those pennies would burn our house down one day, and he spewed out that she had better shut her damn mouth.

In those days, my favorite thing was playing with cousins, so I did not need convincing to visit them. Sam had money, milk cows, and plenty of land for somebody to scream where nobody could hear. On his land, there were places to hide where no one could find me. That is, unless I jumped out and let them.

Grandma's house was next door to Sam and Mattie's house, so grownups would gather there and sit in rockers on her porch, fanning with funeral parlor fans and talking. All us kids played in the yard. I could forget the things that always seemed to be happening at our house, and pretend I was just like my cousins. Free and happy and not scared of anything. Grandma always brought sweet tea to the porch for everybody. Sweetest tea I'd ever tasted, or ever would.

The air hung heavy that night. It felt like lightning was about to strike, but there was no thunder. I was happy, though. I liked everything about that dairy. I could run back and forth between Sam and Mattie's house and Grandma's all day long without giving out. On this night, as always, the grownups sat on the porch, rocking and drinking sweet iced tea and we played in the yard. Daddy and his brothers sounded alike when they belly laughed. The women fanned faster and giggled. They'd say, *Oh, now, you better hush that.* I wasn't worried about a thing because Daddy had no whiskey with him.

I caught sight of a tiny shining light at the edge of the trees growing along the side of the house. Fireflies! Lightning bugs, as we called them then. I loved lightning bugs! Dropping the branch that I had been carrying to poke somebody with, I ran to the porch yelling, "I need a fruit jar, Mama! I need one now!"

As I scrambled up the steps, my foot slipped, and I shaved my shin on the cement edge. It hurt like the dickens, but I ignored the scrape and kept running, demanding that jar. Chasing lightning bugs and putting them in fruit jars was more fun than anything I knew. Something about those little bugs reminded me of how I felt myself. It might have been the way they blinked on and off in their jar jail. They knew they had lost their freedom, but still seemed happy.

I liked to sit on the porch with a flickering jar and talk to the fireflies. It made me feel good, especially when I opened the lid for them to escape. It never failed, but that one of them remained on the bottom as if it wanted to stay. That one little light, in my mind, was me. I would help it out and let it sit in my hand until it got its strength back, and then blow it off my hand. I wanted to cry when it flew away. Sometimes, I thought it might not want to go, either. The other fireflies hurt it, pushing it to the bottom and stepping on it.

Though I was skinny with big scary eyes and a head of straight, black hair that always looked messy, I was tough. Made tough, they said, by my daddy's shenanigans. I tried to be happy when I could because I knew things would cause me to be sad and scared again sooner or later. Life was like the seasons, always changing. My need was to get all the happy I could get whenever possible. Looking back, it would have been nice if someone had figured out a way to help us, but no one ever did.

Mama pushed her glasses up on her nose, the way she did when we frustrated her. "Get on now. I don't have a fruit jar."

I hopped up and down, frantic that the lights would leave before I could get to them. By the time that Grandma said there was a jar in the pantry I could use, I was beside myself. I threw the screen door open and flailed into the house. Just before the BANG, Bang, Bang, bang sound it made when it slammed, Mama screeched, "Don't slam the door!"

She was forever too late in yelling that at us. I often wondered why she even wasted her breath. Mama squawked about something or other all the time, so we tended to ignore her. I regret that now. She had a massive load on her. A young woman tied up with a man as mean as our daddy could be when he was drunk. Three kids that she didn't dare leave with him, but that kept her with him because, how could she leave without them?

I found the jar and hit the door with my palm.

"Don't slam the door …!"

I thought about stopping to ease the door closed but changed my mind. I was set on getting those lightning bugs before they disappeared. They were so beautiful. I needed to watch them go on and off in a jar, then set them free when it was time to go inside and stop looking at them.

Then, out of the night came a soft, good voice. You know the one. It makes you happy just to hear it. My cousin John William called. "Come on, let's play Hide 'n Seek."

That did me in. Running toward the bugs, then toward the cousins, I could not make up my mind. Now and then I would come to a point where it seemed my body ran one way and my mind the other. There was no way I could pull both of them together. There were times I thought I would go stark raving mad right in the middle of that wild confusion.

"Jessie, stop that silliness." Mama fussed.

Knowing that I was going crazy, and not being silly, I tossed the jar and ran to the Hickory tree. Somebody threw a bat; someone else caught it; dirty hands climbed it. My right hand found a narrow slit, but my left one had to scrunch under the lip. I was it!

They scattered. I hated to be it! Everybody knew how to hide better than I could hide and it was so hard to find anybody. I leaned against the tree and sank my face into the crook of a skinny elbow. "One, two, three, four, five, six …" I counted. "One hundred, ready or not, here I come."

In circles, in squares, up the hill, in the ditch, to the back of the house I ran. I saw scampering, heard giggling, found nobody, sat on a stump, and cried. My straight black hair hung in my eyes and my dress stuck to my legs. I was so tired and sweaty it was a relief to hear Mama squeal. "Kids, time to go!"

At last, I could leave them all in hiding places. I headed for the car. Bobby stayed behind until Daddy's voice boomed. "You heard your mama; get in the damn car."

I scrambled into the back seat. Bobby hopped onto the running board pretending he was Superman. His skinny arms crooked skyward as if he thought he had muscles, which he did not.

"Where's your sister?" Daddy glared at us, one at a time. We shrugged, one at a time. Then, he called, "Darcy, get your tail out here."

Darcy slouched from the back of the house, arm in arm with one of our cousins. Face red with anger, embarrassed that he yelled at her, she climbed in next to Mama. Bobby and I settled in the back seat. When he stuck his tongue out at me, I backhanded his head.

"Mama, Jessie hit me."

"Stop it, Jessie; you want the belt?"

"No, Ma'am."

I slumped and crossed my arms across my chest, pouting. I could not believe Bobby had even been born.

Everything was fine before he got here. Every time I looked at his white hair and blue eyes, I gritted my teeth. He had beautiful eyes, and I wanted them. It seemed unfair that he was pretty when he was a boy, and I had to be ugly. I was a girl and supposed to be pretty. I almost talked him into swapping eyes once. I had black hair so I figured his blue eyes would make me look like Elizabeth Taylor. Then, I'd be the prettiest thing in the world. But we had no idea how to get it done. We knew we would have to hide it from Mama and Daddy because they would never let us do anything like that.

Bobby would have done it, though. He got along with everybody, even with me. I hated him most of the time because everybody liked him all the time. They said he was cute and sweet, and precious, and so polite. I don't remember a time anybody saying even one of those things about me. They said I was stubborn and hard to deal with, frustrating and not too cute. Every grownup who ever lived thought Darcy was the prettiest thing they had ever laid eyes on. She had that long red hair and sparkling black eyes. And her skin made her look like a porcelain doll, they said.

I decided to daydream because that was fun. I did it whenever I could. I dreamed about the way my sister's red hair pooled around her white face. It tickled her shoulders and fell on down her back. She was so beautiful the boys said it hurt their eyes to look at her, but she had a hot temper. Once, she tried to hang Curtis for looking up her dress while she was seesawing with Christine. She couldn't tie the rope secure enough, though, so he fell instead of actually hanging. He told everybody she hung him and that it messed up his mind. I guess that was as good a reason as any for the way he acted. Daddy said he had problems in the head before she hung him, that she would have done him a favor if the rope had held.

Thinking about Darcy made me feel homely and sad, though, so my thinking turned to that brother of mine. He was Mama's pet, and I would as soon wring his neck as look at him. My mind wondered to why I looked and acted like me, and why I was born to this family. It felt to me like some other family and not this one should be mine, but it must be so because I looked too much like Daddy. Everybody agreed on that.

My friend Suzy said one day, "Jessie, your hair looks like black sticks blowing in the wind." Mama tried to make my hair look nice but she never could. Darcy's hair was thick and curly, but my hair was straight and thin and so black it looked blue. My ears stuck through it on the sides, too.

People said we had Indian blood running in our veins and that was the reason my hair was so straight and black. I thought about making them take that blood out but also knew it would be a waste of time to ask. My eyes were so big they scared me. Instead of blue like Bobby's eyes or black like Darcy's, they had three colors. Grandma said they were hazel, but I thought that was a woman's name, so it made no sense to me.

Grandma made little sense most of the time, though. She was short, not more than five feet. I wondered if Daddy was hers because he was tall and skinny, but she had to have known she had a baby so I guess he was her child. Her knees and fingers were swollen, with knots on them like on a tree trunk. She waddled when she walked, but she worked hard and never got mad.

I would sit on the screened porch and shuck corn with her while she asked questions about Daddy. She'd ask how he was and if he was still drinking and hitting Mama. I knew she wanted to think he was good, so I lied. I told her he was getting better every day; that they went to the drive-in movie the other night and had a good time. I picked the shucks up when she dropped them because her fat kept her from bending.

The car bumped over something. I hoped it was not a squirrel but I knew that Daddy never swerved to miss the little buggers, sometimes even tried to run over them on purpose. Mama and Daddy were fussing about who gave Grandma the salt and pepper shakers she had used at the supper table. Daddy said they did. Mama said Sam and Mattie had to have because they always did nice things for Grandma. She said Sam knew how to make a living and take care of his family. Daddy spouted off she didn't know what in the hell she was talking about. They talked that way a lot, so I paid little attention to them. Darcy begged them to be quiet. Bobby drew pictures on the car window with his finger. I wanted to find my real family.

It was dark and eerie driving home. I had a strange feeling something was wrong. A bright glow all of a sudden stretched across the sky in front of the car. None of us had ever seen a sight so beautiful. Daddy slowed the car until it crawled to a stop. His voice sounded odd, like the cat with its neck caught in the screen door.

"What'n the hell?"

Mama frowned and pushed at her glasses. "I don't know." It sounded like she knew but didn't want to know that she knew.

Then, Daddy muttered, "Oh, hell," and pushed the accelerator to the floorboard. I fell back against the seat, Bobby down to the floorboard, arms over his head whimpering we were all going to die. The car went fast, but it seemed like slow motion. Dust was all around us, so it was hard to see ahead.

When Mama screamed, I shut my eyes. "It's our house! Oh, my God, our house is on fire!"

Bobby and I grabbed the back of the front seat, and strained to see the beauty of it.

"Great day in the morning!" I whispered.

By that time, our house was a skeleton. Fire lapped, licked, and swirled around it as if the devil was eating it alive. People stood on the side of the road but not too close because of the heat. One man was brave enough to rescue Bobby's scorched bicycle. He darted out of the crowd, jumped on and off the porch with it on his shoulders.

He brought it to Daddy, who took it and muttered, "Thank you kindly." Daddy trembled so hard he had trouble standing, so holding the bicycle steadied him. Mama's hand was shaking so I patted it. She smiled down at me, but there were tears in her eyes.

I remembered the cat and grabbed my chest. At first, my voice was squeaky. When words finally crawled out, they sounded like someone else's words and not my own.

"Where's the cat? Mama, where's the cat?" I poked at her arm, trying to stay calm so I wouldn't scream.

A skinny man said he saw a cat jump out the window and run into the woods and I felt some better. "I bet that cat won't ever stop running." I tried to giggle, but my chin quivered.

Then I remembered my dolls in the big black baby carriage that Santa had brought me; they had been in the house. I looked around for another hero, but there wasn't one. The devil ate my dolls. I screamed inside, but nothing came out. I started to run to the pathetic skeleton, but Mama held me back. "No, hon. You can't go up there; it's too hot. Too late."

"I have to Mama. My babies are in there. They must be hurting. Let me go."

She shook her head and held me back. I had been playing with them, and she had told me to take them in the house. Always wanting things in their proper place. I was furious, and decided I was going to find another family for sure this time. These people burned down houses and killed dolls and cats.

I saw the refrigerator standing in the middle of the charred confusion. It looked like a warrior king. I stopped crying over my babies' suffering and wondered if the butter had melted. Or if it could still be in there, a yellow blob waiting for me to sneak a bite.

"Mama, you reckon the butter's melted?"

She laughed. I never remembered her ever laughing before that night and wondered why.

When the fire truck came, everything was already gone. The firemen squirted water from a big hose for a while, but quit and left, saying they were sorry for our loss. The watchers left, too, one at a time. We stayed in front of the fire, huddled together like a losing football team trying to figure out what to do next. Mama cried because she'd lost her house. For a mama, a house is about all she has. I cried because I lost my dolls and knew I would never see that cat again. Bobby cried because we did, and Darcy always cried or beat me up. I was glad she was crying.

A tear slid down Daddy's face. I saw it. I figured he cried because he had to find another place for us to live. For a daddy, that is one hard job.

"What about the cows, Daddy?" Darcy wrinkled her nose, and I wanted to pinch it.

"Sam'll have to take 'em back. I can't keep 'em. Got to go somewhere and find a job; can't be worrying about no cows right now."

Darcy didn't like his answer because she loved the cows. She would lie down next to them, put her head on their stomachs while they rested, and discuss life with them. She said they responded, but they never said anything to me so I couldn't prove they even knew how to speak.

Once, Darcy put me on Old Jean and left me on her. The cow walked around until I slid off when she stumbled in the creek. I never much liked cows. My favorite were horses.

Daddy said horses made no sense, all they did was eat and sleep, what did I want one for anyway. I wanted one because they were pretty. I wanted to ride out in the pasture and sing, "Happy trails to you" like Dale Evans did in the movies.

Daddy mumbled, "Get in the car." Since we spent little time disobeying him, we got in the car as he commanded. He drove us back to Sam's house, nobody saying a thing until I thought of something important. "Mama, what we gonna wear tomorrow?"

"I don't know." She sounded like she did when Daddy was late for supper. I figured this burned down house thing depressed her. It was sad for us all.

When we got to Sam's house, we had to wake them up to tell them about our fire. We were pitiful. We had no house, and I didn't have any dolls. Mattie made beds in different parts of the house for us. She made a bed for me on the settee where Sam watched ball games. I wanted to be sad about losing our home but wanted to watch Sam's television more. We didn't have one at our old place. We stayed at Sam's house until Daddy found another house to rent closer in to town and we moved again.

People gave us clothes to wear that didn't fit and looked at us funny if we got them dirty. I felt lonely for my own stuff and ugly wearing somebody else's clothes. Their clothes cost more money than our things cost, but I still liked my own stuff better.

We had to go to school in Madison instead of Godfrey and the kids at that school were mean to us, and it was lonely. Bobby sat on the steps looking cute, but nobody said anything to him. They even kicked his feet and ankles when they walked up the steps beside him. He smiled at everybody the way Mama taught us to do. I could see the sad in his eyes, though. I started liking Bobby about then. Darcy acted brave and stood up for us, but I could tell it scared her inside. It had to be hard having to take care of all three of us and not being able to get it done right.

We acted tough and said nothing about school to Mama and Daddy because Mama would cry and Daddy would drink. Darcy and I could hear Bobby sniffling at night, but we let our tears slide down our faces without noise. I pointed my finger at Darcy's back at night so the end of it would touch her so light she wouldn't feel it. I needed to be close to my sister. I thought she might have felt my finger but pretended because she needed to be close, too. But I might have been wrong. I'm not sure about that.

For a little while I was mad at God. I knew enough about Him to know that He could have stopped that fire before it burned everything up. Grandma said He was the one who made me in the first place, so I had no business telling Him what to do with things He made. I had no right being angry with Him. She said He could do anything He wanted with anybody He wanted.

I apologized to Him at some point, but something happened to me after that fire. I stopped running and playing games with cousins. I even stopped chasing fireflies. I felt older than my actual age, and all beat up, like that lightning bug on the bottom of the jar. I no longer sang about Buggerbears and never played the game again.

We lived in Madison for a while but Daddy gave the cows back to Sam because he had no place to keep them. He had no job to feed our faces for a while. Then he heard about a big new plant in the next state, South Carolina, and said he would try for a job there. He left us for a few months to fend for ourselves so he could get a job and come back for us. It was a hard time, but we did okay. He did come back one day, though, and packed us up so we could move.

When we left Madison, we didn't look out the back window to see it getting smaller as we drove away. We had always liked to do that. We knew we'd left our cousins, the cows, the games and fun of all the years. But nobody there seemed to care much what we did so we decided we wouldn't care, either. We knew we only had each other, not even Grandma. It was hard to swallow when I thought about it, but it was what I had to do.

I pushed the Buggerbears down inside and told them to stay there. They were never to bother me anymore. I knew without wondering that Daddy couldn't kill them. He had worries of his own.

Aunt Mattie said it was as if our family fell off the face of the earth. She said nobody heard anything from us for years, but if anybody tried to find us, we knew nothing about it. I missed Mattie more than cousins, or games, or cows, or even my dolls.

She told me later that she was hanging clothes on the clothesline one day when a voice behind her spoke.

"Hey, Mattie."

She said she turned around and looked into the face of the sweetest child she had ever known who'd now grown up. A woman with jet black hair and a smile so bright one might think they saw an angel, stood before her. Mattie said the woman's eyes were soft and tender, the prettiest color of hazel she'd ever seen, and she knew those eyes.

"Oh, my Lord! Jessie!"

Grandma's Favorite

She loves me, she loves me not.

She loves me, she loves me not.

When Grandma called, "Jessie, get a pail and a paper sack and come on out to the screen porch," I dropped the jump rope and scurried to the pantry for a pail, trying not to make a mess. I headed for the porch where Grandma perched like a soft, plump pillow in a straight-back chair, pail resting in her lap, floor covered with corn picked from Papa's garden. I was scrawny but lugged a stool up next to her and grinned. Grandma was so sweet it hurt my heart.

"When you peel corn, do you find worms like I do, Grandma?" I yanked half a worm from the corn and tossed it into the shuck bag.

Grandma's voice sounded like static on the radio when the station was having trouble coming through. "I sure do, hon, but the worms need food, too, and corn's what God gives 'em to eat."

Strands of graying hair frizzled from the bun on the back of her round head, framing her cheeks like a haze around a full moon. In all her life, Grandma had never trimmed her hair, and evenings when she let it down to brush, she would let us grandkids handle it. It felt like cool water running through my fingers when I touched it.

Grandma brushed the ringlets away from her face with the back of her hand and prattled on about how summer made folks sluggish and how many dairy cows Sam had to milk with no help. She said it sure was hard to find good help these days, but I didn't know why. I had faith in her, though, and let it go at that.

"Jessie! Let's play something; I'm bored." Ben called from the back yard.

"I'm busy peeling corn with Grandma, thank you anyway." I smiled at Grandma.

"Peeling corn?" Ben was resentful when I was alone with Grandma, and knowing it agitated him made me feel I was the most beloved of Grandma's grandchildren, and that excited me.

"Grandma asked me to." I smiled again. She winked a glittering brown eye my way.

"Grandma? Which one of us do you love the best?"

I tried to act laid back, but it was vital that I know the answer to that question. Adults did not often say they much liked me, so Grandma choosing me was important. Ben believed he was her favorite and all the time told me that he was. I wanted him to know he was dead wrong for once in my life.

"Now, Jessie. I love you all." Her distorted fingers tugged at the shucks.

"Does peeling corn hurt your fingers, Grandma?"

"Sometimes it does a little bit, but it ain't bad."

"How come they're big like that?" I motioned with my head toward the gnarled fingers.

Grandma released the corn and held her hands out in front of her, turning them this way and that. "I don't rightly know. Probably arthritis."

"What's that?"

"Just old age, hon."

"Does everybody get old age hands?"

"I reckon so."

I did not appreciate that answer in the least. Grandma didn't often say such things, either, because she knew how much I would dread from then on having lumps on my fingers. I always took everything to heart as if it was going to happen to me, too, if it had happened to anybody else, especially bad things.

"I don't want to hear you talk like that, Grandma."

"I'm just telling the truth. Don't you want to hear the truth?"

"No, Ma'am." I jutted my bottom lip out to show how serious I was.

Grandma chuckled, and I felt better. I determined to shift the subject to something else so I wouldn't hear about things I didn't want to hear about, but Ben suddenly exploded through the screen door, scowling at me.

"That's my stool, ignoramus. Give it."

"It ain't yours. I use it when I help Grandma peel corn."

"You're dumb, Jessie. You don't peel corn; you shuck it."

"Well … well, you can shuck it if you want to; I peel it." I lifted my nose like the women I had seen in the movies.

Peeling sounded much better than shucking. Besides, my daddy said a word like that when he had been drinking, and it didn't seem pleasurable. It also made my mama cry and my brother hide under the bed.

Grandma looked from one of us to the other, her eyes shimmering the way they did when something pleased her. I could not imagine what pleased her, though, what with Ben frustrating me so intolerably.

"Go away, Ben; we're busy." I thought I sounded in charge, capturing it in my ears.

"You don't belong here, Jessie; go on back to Atlanta. This is my home."

"It ain't yours. It's Grandma's."

Ben shoved me from the stool so hard I splayed spread-eagled on top of the corn and Grandma scowled but didn't fuss at him. That hurt my feelings. I tried to clamber back on the stool, but he snatched it from me and sat on it himself.

"Get off it, Ben!" I bellowed, furious at his behavior.

Grandma knew that if Ben did not listen to me, I would end up having to cuff him across the head and force him off the stool. He was a year older and a lot bigger, and would most likely punch me back, so the thought made me nervous. But Daddy said a person should never take back his word, and my word was for Ben to get off the stool. He had to get off because I could not take back my word. I had to do what I said, or Daddy would see to it I never said anything like that again.

"Ben, let Jessie use the stool. You can use it any day, but she ain't here often, and I want you to treat her nice."

He grumbled but got off the stool, then angrily shoved it at me. I knew by the way he frowned that he planned on settling the score. I would need some time to figure out how to get around his plans, whatever they would be.

All of a sudden, it came to me. "You better not be planning nothing bad, Ben, or I'll tell Darcy on you."

The look on his face proved I had won the skirmish. All the cousins were afraid of Darcy because they knew she would hurt them. On top, again, I was number one in many ways.

At supper, Aunt Mattie tittle tattled about a woman in town she said was running around with the banker. Uncle Sam warned her she had best mind her own business or she would end up in hot water herself. Ben and Beth frowned at each other and at me. My hands were raw from shucking corn, but I felt good about Grandma making Ben leave us alone together.

Darcy didn't much like visiting at Sam and Mattie's but Mama and Daddy needed to work on things, they said, so they made her stay. Bobby stayed at Uncle Clyde's and Aunt Wilma's because they had all boys.

However, it irritated Darcy because she liked to play with those cousins best. She sulked, dropping her head so that her big red hair hung in her face. Mattie told her to tuck it behind her ears so it wouldn't get in her mouth when she ate, but Darcy said, "I ain't gonna, and you can't make me."

Mattie said all right and passed the food, all the time trying to make everybody eat seconds. Ben stared at me until I was too nervous to eat.

"I can't eat any more, Mattie." I tried to smile sweetly, the way I knew Mattie liked smiles. She nodded, and let me be excused. I left the room and went to the front porch where I could sit on the glider and push the floor with my toes to make it swing. Ben followed and sat down beside me. I refused to look at him.

He lowered his husky voice just about to a whisper and put his mouth close to my ear. "You better stop shucking corn with my Grandma."

"Oh, yeah?" My voice sounded weak. "What you gonna do about it if I don't?" My heart pounded in my chest so hard I thought I could see it beating.

"You better stop it now, or you'll find out what I'm gonna do to you, ugly city girl."

I hated to be called city girl. Ben called me ugly all the time, but it didn't bother me because I was used to that. It got to me, though, when he called me a city girl. Daddy said people would try to get to you but that you should never let them know it if they did because they would never by God stop if you let them know. Still, no matter how hard I tried to ignore Ben, I couldn't stop thinking about that.

"I can't help it because I'm from the city. I didn't ask to be born there. You're just jealous anyway."

The two of us pushed the glider with our feet, saying nothing until Darcy came out, shoved Ben out of his seat, and sat down in his place.

"Darcy, you better stop being mean to me." His voice sounded like a baby squirrel fussing at intruders.

She squinted and gave him her most mean look. He couldn't look her in the eyes when she narrowed them like that. The last time he had crossed her, she tried to flush his head down the commode, and he came near to drowning.

"Darcy, Ben said I can't help Grandma peel corn or sit on my stool."

"It ain't yours, moron."

Darcy balled her fist, but he defended his head so she couldn't clobber him. She horse-laughed and called him a scared cat. "Scared cat; scared cat!" She howled.

"I'm telling." He ran into the house sniveling.

"Go ahead, scared cat. See if I care." She swung harder. Darcy and I grinned at each other, knowing we had the upper hand, something else Daddy said; a person had better keep the upper hand.

Ben didn't tattle on Darcy, but the next morning he had gone up to Grandma's house before I was out of bed. I gulped my food to get up there before he had time to turn her against me. When I reached the kitchen door, I heard Ben whimpering how he was good all the time and she ought to treat him better than she treated me. I peered through the rusty screen and saw Grandma hug him. Something in my chest started to hurt like somebody was squeezing me too hard.

"Ben," Grandma cooed, "You got to understand. Poor little Jessie and Darcy and Bobby got a hard life back home, what with their daddy being the black sheep and all. I just feel like I ought to try and take up the slack when they're here."

"You mean I'm still your favorite grandchild; you just act to Jessie like I ain't?"

My heart fell apart there on the spot, like the puzzles I tried to tote to Mama so she could see how good I was at putting them together. Grandma looked at Ben with so much love in her eyes, I thought it must be like that up in Heaven.

"You'll always be my favorite grandchild when you're with me, Ben. But when Jessie's helping me shuck corn, she's my favorite right then."

I could tell Ben didn't understand what she was actually saying. I didn't understand, and I was smart for my age.

"How can both of us be your favorite?" He sounded down, and there I went, feeling sorry for the boy. I shook my head to get those sad feelings out of my brain.

"All of you are my grandchildren, and I love every one of you just the same. It's just that when one is with me, I love that one best right then. I can't love one more than I love another. Every one of you is so special it makes me want to cry."

Ben nodded as if he understood, but I knew that he didn't. He would accept what she said because, like me, he trusted Grandma. I didn't like it much, though, because I thought she should love me the most even when I wasn't with her. I once heard someone say that absence makes the heart grow fonder, but Mama added: "for somebody else." I didn't believe her when she said it, but here was my own Grandma, saying the same thing.

I sneaked away like a mouse in the dark and didn't tell anybody what I had heard. I wasn't sure what to say anyway since I had no idea what a black sheep was. The only ones I had ever seen were white, so how was I to know about black sheep? It didn't seem fair that Grandma loved Ben the best when I was not there. I didn't visit often. That meant she loved Ben more than me. "I ain't gonna peel corn with her no more, then." I had made up my mind.

I was sitting on the glider when Ben ran by, slapped me on the shoulder, and chirped, "Grandma wants to see you." He seemed content. Well, of course, I would be, too, if I was Grandma's favorite the most times.

I mulled it over and then decided it wasn't Ben's fault. Grandma was the one loving or not loving people. It made more sense to be upset with her. That way, I would have a reason not to peel corn with her any longer. I didn't like it much anyhow; it made my fingers sore.

I trudged up the trail and walked into her kitchen. "You want me, Grandma?" I didn't smile and let my voice drag so she would know I was unhappy with her. Even rolled my eyes and sighed for effect, the way Darcy always did with Mama. Grandma flashed her sparkling smile my way, so it was hard not to smile back at her.

"I sure do, Jessie. Want to help me churn for buttermilk before you go home?" She raised her little black eyebrows.

My heart bloomed like a rose right there in that kitchen. Grandma wanted me to help her churn, which meant she loved me best, right then and there. I could hardly wait to get the other churn from the pantry and pull up a chair next to my Grandma. It was glorious to be loved by her. Ben didn't own her love right then. I did.

This was worth the world to me. I beamed and chugged, and when Grandma's eyes twinkled at me, I decided to make the most of our time together while I was her favorite.

"Grandma? Want me to tell you some secret things about me? Then you can love me when I'm not here."

Kids and Young Ladies

*Beth had more clothes
than any girl could ever possibly wear.*

Every summer when I visited, I asked to borrow something, and every summer she said I could not, would not, never could, and never would.

The prettiest things she had were fuzzy sweaters wrapped in plastic bags and stored in her bureau. Several times I got as far as opening the drawer and touching a bag before she caught me. But up to that fateful day, I was never able to feel one.

She said they were cashmere and I was never to put my grubby paws on them. Aunt Mattie told me they were angora, but not to tell Beth because she would never wear them if she knew. I didn't know why that was. Things were never explained to me, just told.

One day, I saw Aunt Mattie taking a cardigan and some other sweaters to the giveaway pile (the place where they put clothes for the less fortunate) so I sidled up to her, one finger twiddling at the pullover she held. I asked why she was putting them in the giveaway pile and she said Beth got stains on them and didn't want them any longer.

I had to keep wearing my clothes whether they had stains on them or not. Sometimes they had big, brown ones on them and Mama had to throw them away. But we never had anything left over for the less fortunate.

I wanted to ask Aunt Mattie if she would let me have one, that I would wear it even with the stain. It wouldn't matter to me. But she drove away before I mustered up the nerve to ask.

Beth had a date one night, so I decided to get in that drawer while she was gone. I spent half the night taking sweaters out, pulling them from their bags, and rubbing them on my face. Never in my life had I felt anything as soft or smelled anything more pleasing. Once finished, I tried to put them back the way I found them, but when I closed the drawer, a tiny pink sliver stuck out. No matter how hard I tried, I could not get that pink piece of the sweater to stay in the drawer. The more I tried, the more nervous I became until, too sleepy to worry about it, I gave up and climbed into bed.

The next morning, I was in the kitchen asking Aunt Mattie questions when Beth screamed so loud it hurt my eardrums. It sounded as if someone was killing her, so we ran to her room. She was standing in the middle of the room, pointing at the piece of pink sticking out of the drawer.

"Mummy!" She howled, looking at me, then at the pink material. "She touched my sweaters!"

Aunt Mattie glanced first at the drawer, then at me. I knew she was disappointed in me, but I didn't think what I'd done was all that bad. I hadn't hurt them.

I swallowed. "I just felt 'em. I didn't get 'em dirty."

"What am I going to do? Now, I have no sweaters to wear."

I looked at Beth. "How come you can't wear 'em? They ain't dirty."

I could not believe how she was carrying on. Sweaters weren't anything that significant, like cows you had to keep to milk. Now, those cows would matter if something happened to them.

"In the light of eternity, Beth, all this ain't necessary." I didn't exactly know what that meant, but Mama said it all the time, so I figured it fit the moment.

She glared at me. "Not necessary? Jessie Mae, you touched my sweaters with your dirty hands. I most certainly will not wear them after such abuse."

"They ain't nothing but clothes. You don't make no sense." I turned and left the room, angry that she thought my hands were dirty. They looked clean to me. Besides, I washed them before I got into her bureau drawer.

Beth whined until Sam said she had to give the sweaters to the family in the farmhand house. He felt they could use them if she had to be such a ninny; I didn't do anything to the sweaters just because I touched them; I wasn't no animal. I loved Sam more than ever when he said that to her. Over and over, I had dreamed of him being my daddy. Beth should have to be in my place sometimes, I thought. She wouldn't act like such a snit then.

I was disappointed that Aunt Mattie agreed with Beth, but guess she had to, what with Beth being her own child and all. Uncle Sam said it was dumb paying real money for clothes when people in other countries were starving. If Beth wanted something, though, it didn't matter how many hungry people there were, Aunt Mattie got it for her.

Beth ranted a long time when Sam took her sweaters and came back without them. She cried all day, wouldn't even get out of her room for supper. Aunt Mattie made ice cream and cookies for her later. I felt sorry that I'd made her so unhappy. I hadn't meant for all that to happen. All I'd wanted was to feel those sweaters. They had felt like sweet baby rabbits before people killed them for their feet.

When I thought about that, I remembered Aunt Mattie warning me not to tell Beth that they were angora. I didn't know what angora was, but I did know it felt like rabbits. I'd felt them before. Daddy kept them for pets; at least, that's what he said. I'm not sure he was telling the whole truth about that. They'd disappear from time to time, and later we'd see what looked like it might be them on the serving plate at the supper table. I couldn't eat those nights.

I knocked lightly on Beth's door, and she mumbled something, so I opened it and whispered her name.

"What do you want?"

"Can I talk to you?"

"Go away. I don't like you right now."

"Beth, I'm sorry for what I did. Can I come in and talk, please?"

I don't want to talk. Go away."

"Please. I'll make it up to you, I promise."

"Yeah? You'll do whatever I ask?"

"Uh huh, I'll do whatever you want me to do."

"Okay, come in then."

I stepped inside and stood against the door. Beth was

sitting in the middle of the bed; legs crossed, eyes swollen, face red and splotched, smirking at me. I felt awful that I'd caused her to look so horrible.

Edging to the bed, I asked, "Will you forgive me?"

"I got a date tonight, and I want you to double date with us. Then I'll think about forgiving you." She grinned like she had something up her sleeve that was going to be unpleasant for me.

"Sure!"

I'd never had a date before and here she was, forgiving me this quick. A date! How could life be better than this? I forgot to doubt her.

Beth let me wear her clothes to look more grown up. She was almost four years older than I was and it scared me a little to think about dating a boy that old since I'd never dated one at all. But I trusted Beth. She said he'd be fun and would teach me about boy and girl dating.

"What if Mama and Daddy find out?"

"Don't worry about that. Nobody'll tell 'em."

Aunt Mattie stuck her head in the door. "The boys are here!"

Suddenly I was a nervous wreck. Beth's clothes

were too big and had pointed places on the front that stuck out and looked strange. It seemed weird with makeup on my face; not at all like me, and I didn't know if I should smile or if it might crack my face. I also felt guilty. I knew Mama and Daddy would be upset if they knew about this. But it was too late to worry about it. Those boys were here already.

"I can't do it, Beth. I can't! I can't!"

I thought I was going to explode, start screaming and running in circles. My feet were jumping all around the room even though I wasn't telling them to.

"Jessie Mae, you said you'd do it, so you've got to do it. Now, get yourself together. Straighten up, right now. Do you hear me?"

She was serious, shaking her finger at my nose so hard I could feel the air it generated. I nodded. My mind told me not to go because Mama and Daddy would find out and kill me, but Beth shoved me down the hall and into the living room to face the cutest boy I'd ever seen.

Music came from somewhere. Things moved in slow motion, air flowed around me like a warm, swirling ocean, soft and gentle on my legs. I was in love even before he took my hand and led me out the door. My life would never be the same again. My mind whirled as I tried to think of how I could get Mama and Daddy to let me live here for the rest of my time on earth.

Beth and Larry sat in the front seat because he was old enough to drive. He didn't seem to mind how close she was to him, but I couldn't figure out how he could drive with her under him like that

I couldn't think of anything to say. I guess Kenneth couldn't, either, because he scrunched against his door and I sat against my door, our hands tight in our laps. Now and then, we'd glance at each other and smile. He had bright white teeth. I wondered if he'd ever worn braces. If he had, it would mean his family had lots of money. Braces cost too much for poor people, so I was so lucky to have big, straight teeth.

I had no idea what the movie was about with all the thumping and pumping my heart was doing. All I could think about was that boy in the back seat with me, and I knew that I'd die soon if somebody didn't do something to help me. Suddenly, Kenneth spoke, and the sound of his high-low mixed up voice startled me.

"What did you say?"

I knew that my eyes were too big, but he'd have to

accept me that way. I was too young to make them slant like the women on television when they looked at handsome men.

"I said, you look mighty pretty tonight." He smiled again, and my whole body shivered. "You cold?"

"Oh, God, I'm going to die," was all I could think to say, and had trouble not saying it aloud. I nodded to his cold question, then shook my head no. I didn't know if I was cold or not. I was shivering, but it didn't feel like cold shivers. I wanted Mama. I knew I'd feel better with her there. As a matter of fact, I wouldn't have minded Daddy being there. I needed somebody to get me out of this mess.

I smiled my sweetest smile, knowing it was pretty with all Beth's makeup, and with a big smile, I'd be the most gorgeous girl he'd ever seen. I guess I was.

He made one huge hop, and I could smell his breath and perfume, even though boys were not supposed. to wear perfume. Just knowing that he wore it made me not like him as much. He was looking plainer by the minute.

That boy wrapped his skinny arms around me and jerked me to him. Before I could let my breath back out, he put his mouth on top of mine and mashed it hard. I didn't like it one little bit. Daddy said I wasn't to let people bully me, and this boy was bullying me badly, so I hauled off and knocked the daylights out of his head with my fist.

He jumped back. "What'd you do that for?" He looked so surprised I thought about laughing but decided not to.

"You ain't supposed to do that to nobody if you ain't been asked to, stupid."

Beth and Larry heard the commotion and turned around. When she saw my face, her eyes grew big, and her mouth dropped open for speaking, but it was too late. I lit into Kenneth with words I'd learned from my daddy when he was drunk. I could hear them coming out, but I couldn't stop them. Part of me didn't even want to. When I'd finished, he was sitting on the other side of the seat wearing the palest face I'd ever seen. His white smile was gone.

I sank back, crossed my arms and pouted. "I wanna go home, Beth." I glared at her. When she didn't respond but kept staring at me with that open mouth, I repeated my sentence, this time adding "and I don't wanna have to say it again." I knew that part of a sentence always got me moving when Daddy said it. I hoped it would work with her, and it did. Nobody said a word on the way home, and when we got there, I jumped out before the car stopped rolling, ran to

Beth's room and fell across the bed sobbing. Her makeup messed up her white bedspread, and I dared her to say anything about it, or I'd make her eat it.

She touched my arm. "Jessie, I didn't mean for anything bad to happen. I'm sorry."

"How come you do something like that to me? I trusted you."

"Why do you think I did it to be mean?"

"Cause you did, Beth. You're mean as a snake. You knew I didn't know nothing about dating. How come you let him do that to me?"

"All he did was try to kiss you. I know you're too young for that kind of stuff, but it ain't all that bad. Besides, he didn't really do it, did he?"

I fell back on the bed, arm over my forehead. "How in the world can you say it ain't that bad?"

I sat up, fixed my eyes on hers, hands on my hips. "Don't you understand nothing? He was trying to bully me, and Daddy said that was a bad thing for people to do. I think he got close enough for me to get pregnant."

I raised my eyebrows two times fast. "And there ain't no way in hell I can have no baby when I'm too young to even date."

She was quiet. I watched her face go from trying to figure out what I was saying to half-knowing, to total knowing.

"Oh, good grief, Jessie! You can't get babies by kissing."

"You can't?" I had never felt such relief in all my life.

Beth rummaged in a dresser drawer and pulled out a huge book with pictures in it. When she'd finished explaining the facts of life to me, I felt better. At least I wouldn't be thrown out of the house for being a slut, what Mama called girls who didn't have a husband before they got that way.

I washed my mouth until it felt clean enough and we went to bed. We lay in the dark, Beth explaining over and over how a girl gets pregnant. It was an enlightening evening, and by the time I fell asleep, I knew I was no longer a kid. I was now a young lady. I knew, as well, that I never wanted to have a baby. That sounded like a dreadful thing to happen to a person. And those pictures would not get out of my head.

The next morning, when I looked in the mirror I was surprised. I'd always thought that when I became a young lady, I'd be as beautiful as the women Mama read about in her magazines. But all I saw was a skinny kid with nothing at the top. How could I be almost grown up with nothing at the top?

I thought, too, I would now have to give up kid things and act the Beth and Darcy usually acted. I hated the thought of that, always crying or pouting about something or other, whining in those nasal voices they had. They slept late in the mornings, too, and Mama fussed at Darcy because she never got her chores done because of sleeping so late. Aunt Mattie didn't fuss at Beth for sleeping late because black boys from town did her work for her.

I trudged into the kitchen instead of running in, since I was now a young lady and not a kid who bounces into rooms. I wanted to skip and scare Uncle Sam, but a girl would never do that, only a kid. Aunt Mattie gazed at me.

"You feeling all right, darling?"

"Yes'm." I half-smiled at her, slid on my back in the chair and sighed. I didn't even want to eat I was so frustrated. Being a young lady when I looked and felt like a kid, was not something I considered enjoyable. I didn't like boys that much, anyhow, especially since that horrible episode with that smiling perfumed boy. I looked at Beth slurping her food like a kid.

"Beth, you ought not to slurp your food like that. You ain't no kid no more."

I thought she was going to throw the plate at me, it made her so angry, but it certainly escaped me as to why she was mad. I figured it was the turning from kid to young lady stuff again.

Sam wasn't paying much attention to us, just eating because he had work to do on the farm when he finished. I decided that, since Mama wasn't here for me to talk to, and Aunt Mattie would just say "how nice" no matter what I said, and Uncle Sam was a man and men didn't listen to women, I needed someone to talk to.

Sadie was washing dishes and humming, so I stayed in the kitchen after breakfast to ask her questions. She was good to give honest answers. The most honest person I'd ever known in my whole life. Sadie didn't hurt my feelings being honest, either. She was sweet about it. She never had been one to think down on anybody else, even if they did wrong things. She'd say they must have had a reason or they couldn't help the way they were raised.

I wished a lot of times that I could get away with things because of the way I was raised, but that never worked with Mama. I'd get a spanking every time. Like the time that I ignored her about sitting on the rock under the fig tree and eating figs. She said there were snakes under the rock and I didn't believe her. I thought she wanted to save the figs for preserves, so I sneaked. Two things happened. Something wiggled near my foot, and when I looked down, a baby snake squiggled from underneath the rock and wrapped around my ankle. By the time that I'd stopped screaming Mama was there, fussing about me never minding.

"I ought to beat you right here and now, Jessie Mae. You're just rebellious. I told you a thousand times not to come out here and sit on this rock; you could've been bit and dead before I got out here." Her face was red, red, red.

Second thing lasted until the next day. The figs made me so sick, I thought I'd die, and Mama said every bit of it was deserved. I never forgot about needing to be more careful when Mama told me to do or not to do something. She was the right one in our family, that's for sure.

When everybody but me had left the kitchen, Sadie looked at me and grinned, hands on her aproned hips. "Why you still sittin' here, girl?"

I knew she knew what I wanted, but she was going to make me tell her. She wasn't one to speak for other people.

"I need to talk, Sadie."

I tried to say it the way Daddy would, but my voice was shaky. Besides, I couldn't fool her. Daddy told me that she was as smart as they come, for a black lady. She sat down and looked at me, still smiling that sweet smile of hers. I couldn't imagine life without Sadie, even if I did see her only in the summer.

"Sadie, I think I'm a young lady and not a kid no more." I took a breath and waited.

"And what makes you think that, child?"

"Well, last night I went on a date with Beth and Larry. With a boy (adding in a whisper)."

She put the dishrag in front of her face like she was trying to hide something.

"A boy, huh?"

I nodded at her. "This boy was older than me, and he did something, too."

She cocked her head to the side. "What he go and do? He done kiss you, girl?"

I thought I'd die of embarrassment. I nodded again but kept my eyes down.

"Laws, girl, a kiss don't make you no young lady. Age make you that. You still a kid down in that little heart, ain't you?"

I looked up at her, sunshine peeking through the dark.

"Well, you ain't old enough yet to be no young lady. Now you just quit thinking too much and get on out and play. You're a kid, girl. You're just a little kid with too much thinking time and skinny legs that need to go running. Go on, now." She fluttered the dishrag at me.

I flew to the door, my heart renewed. Sadie never lied so I knew that I must be still a kid and it felt wonderful.

When I got to the door, I met Uncle Sam and stopped. I grinned up at him. He looked down at me, scowling as if he were about to reprimand me. Then, all of a sudden, his false teeth jumped out at me. I screamed and ran, as he howled in laughter.

I sure was glad that kids and young ladies ain't the same and that I was still a kid. I loved Uncle Sam and his jumping teeth. It sure would be a shame if I couldn't scream and run like a scared chicken when they jumped out at me. It sure would be a shame.

Love's Teeth

It was a hot day. The kind that made Grandma sit in a rocker on the porch and fan her fatness with a funeral parlor fan.

As I limped across the gravel between her house and Uncle Sam and Aunt Mattie's place, trying not to hurt my feet, I waved at her. She fluttered her fan at me.

"Morning, Jessie! Come sit a spell with me."

"I'm coming, Grandma!"

On the porch, a dusty ceiling fan moved the air around just enough to keep a person from suffocating in the southern heat. Grandma handed me a fan with a picture of Jesus on it, his arms spread out. I plunked in the rocker next to her. Grandma was good at letting me sit and think, and not making me talk if I didn't want to, so she was comfortable to be around. Not like Granny, my mama's mama.

Granny made me nervous. She was forever trying to feel me, to find out if I was getting to that age yet, whatever that age meant. And she forever warned me to wear girdles so boys would have trouble getting to me. She made no sense to me whatsoever.

"Grandma, do you believe in Heaven?"

"I sure do, child. What makes you ask that?"

"I've been wondering 'bout it some. Seems like there couldn't be another place pretty as Morgan, or as much fun, but Darcy said there was, and it was Heaven. Must be a mighty pretty place, Heaven." I sighed.

Darcy was three and one half years older than I was and talked all the time about Heaven, and how she was going and I was not because, she said, I was not good enough to live there. It scared me when she said it, but I tried not to let her bother me. Most of the time it worked. Of course, every Sunday morning she was faithful and walked down the road to a little church, and I didn't, so she could be right about things. I don't know.

"Jessie, I think Heaven will be even prettier than Morgan. I sure do."

"Jessie! Jessie!" We stopped rocking so we could hear what Mattie was calling about.

"Yes'm!" I stretched my neck to help me hear.

"How 'bout running down to the barn and telling Sam to come for breakfast, darling."

"Yes'm!" I loved helping Mattie. She was the sweetest person in the whole world, and she called me darling, even when she was fussing at me. She was a little plump and short, and I didn't normally like fat people or short people, but she was still my favorite aunt. I loved the way she kept her brown hair curled in tight little ringlets against her head. She made them that way with bobby pins at night. Mama's hair fell all around her face and shoulders in big black puffs and got in her mouth when she turned too fast. Mattie's never did that.

Sometimes, I wished Mattie had been my mother, but then I'd feel guilty and ask God to forgive me and not punish me for thinking such a horrible thought. I loved my mama. I wouldn't have swapped her for another mama, and she was so beautiful. But Aunt Mattie was different. People said she put on, but she was just made that way. I guess they were jealous and that's why they said mean things about her. Mattie liked me, and anyone who did deserved someone to defend them, so that's what I spent a lot of my time doing every summer at Uncle Sam's dairy.

"I'll be back, Grandma; I gotta go get Sam."

She smiled. "All right, Hon."

I loved running. Sweet, warm air rushing through my thin, straight hair, the feel of the ground slapping at my feet but barely touching them, gave me a feeling of invincibility. Mama said I was born running and I think she was right.

Fetching Sam for breakfast was a daily routine when I visited, and I cherished it. Mattie let me do whatever I wanted until time to eat, then sent me hightailing it to the barn for Sam. Then we'd sit around their big kitchen table eating a feast that made me feel like a princess.

"Sam! Sam!" I hollered his name over and over long before I reached the barn, but when I rounded the end of the long building and slid into the door onto the cement aisle, it startled him.

"What in the!" He grabbed his chest and pushed his hat back on his curly head. Sam was the most handsome uncle I had, except for J.W. who was on Mama's side, so that didn't count.

"Great day in the morning, Jessie! You scared the dickens out of me. I swear, girl, you're gonna be the death of me yet."

I giggled. "Mattie said to come to breakfast." I was out of breath, grinning, and hopping up and down by now because I'd stopped running and wanted to start back again. He laughed aloud. The sound made me happy, but I didn't know why. "All right. Tell her I'm on my way."

I whirled and headed back, forgetting that my bare feet did not like the gravel.

In the kitchen, Mattie was putting big trays of food on the table, and cousins were milling about, dragging words like slow wagons behind them. Ben and Beth moped about, scowling and shoving back and forth. I never did know why they were so hateful to each other. If I'd had a home like they had, and a mama and daddy like theirs, I'd be the happiest person on this side of Heaven. I decided they'd been spoiled and thought more of themselves than they ought to think. That's what Mama said, so it must have been the truth.

Sadie was a short black lady, not much bigger than I was, but old, at least as old as Mama and Mattie, and Sadie Mae was her girl. She was Beth's age, three and one half years older than me. Beth and Darcy were the same age, but they didn't like each other much and fussed, so I got along better with Beth than Darcy did, even though that wasn't saying much.

Sadie and Sadie Mae lived in town and came out to the dairy every morning to take care of everybody. Sadie helped Mattie with the cooking. She cleaned house and shucked corn and worked in the garden, and anywhere else that needed working. She ran the house, but she let Mattie think everything was her idea. Sadie Mae ran Beth's bath water, combed her hair and turned back her bed for her to crawl into at night. When I was there, she did those things for me, too, and I couldn't believe that life could be so good.

I'd make believe I lived on a southern plantation because that's the way it felt for me, pretending my name was Scarlet, and I was beautiful. We didn't have people like Sadie and her girl at our house. Mama did all our work. She even combed her own hair; mine, too.

When Sam came in from the barn, we gathered around the table, except for Sadie and Sadie Mae, who took their plates to the screened porch. I never did understand why they didn't eat at the big table with the rest of us, but I also knew not to ask why they didn't. It was understood, somebody once said. I don't remember who said it. I just knew not to be snoopy about other people's business. That was rude. I was hungry and reached for the eggs, but Mattie stopped me.

"Wait for the blessing, darling."

I thought I'd starve if we had to wait too long. I stared at Sam. He lowered his head. Everybody else bowed their heads. I kept staring at him, hoping he'd get it over with in a hurry so we could eat. Suddenly, he raised his head and looked directly at me. His teeth jumped out of his mouth like they were alive and going to eat me right then and there. I screamed and screamed and screamed until Ben shoved me out of the chair.

"Stop yelling, stupid."

"Oh, my gracious! What in the world's the matter, Jessie?"

Mattie looked like she'd seen a mouse, and was holding her chest like she felt faint.

"Mattie," I whined, "Sam stuck his teeth out at me." I whimpered until she got up and soothed my fears, then I sat down, pouting. Sam threw his head back, and belly laughed his good laugh, but I was not going to be happy about it this time.

"Jessie, you're so dumb," Ben called me names all the time, his face screwed up in its sour look. He was fat to me, but Mama said he was just big for his age and could carry extra weight. I wondered if he had any eyebrows because his curly black hair tumbled down and hid them if he had any.

"Takes a dummy to know one."

I stuck out my tongue, the meanest thing I could think of doing. When Ben did the same to me, Mattie sent him from the table until he could act like a gentleman. I guess he decided not to act like one because he didn't come back. Beth shot her disapproval look at me.

Darcy said Beth was a snot, and that's why she didn't like to visit her, but I wanted Beth to be my friend. Darcy said that was because I was a snot, too, but I thought it was because Beth was beautiful and she also had fuzzy sweaters that I liked to touch, and hoped to wear someday.

I let huge, warm tears roll out of my eyes and dangle on the end of my nose. That always worked with Mattie; this day was no different. "Oh, now, darling, don't you go feeling unhappy. Sam, now you say the blessing and let's get on eating. You've scared poor Jessie enough for today."

Sam obeyed her, and we ate. I almost felt bad about being the cause of Ben having to leave the table, but decided he deserved it for looking so mad all the time, and for always calling me names. Beth would pout with me for the rest of the day, so that meant I had to either go to Grandma's and talk with her, find Sadie, or follow Mattie around while she worked. Sadie Mae wouldn't speak to me if Beth wouldn't. She was Beth's person and had to stick up for her whether she wanted to or not. That's just the way it was.

It was a pretty dreary day. For a while, I shucked corn on the porch with Sadie. Those times with her were special times. I could ask her anything I wanted, and she'd answer every one in her slow, relaxed manner. I didn't stay in the garden too long, though, because the heat made me sweat and I didn't like to sweat. It made me squiggly and squishy. I followed Mattie around and talked about Mama and Daddy, Darcy and Bobby, and she asked questions and smiled and said "how nice" every time I said something about them. But I didn't feel like she much cared. Mama said Mattie was jealous, so that was probably why she wasn't interested. After a while, I went to Grandma's.

Papa and Grandma were in the bedroom talking when I went to the back door, so they didn't hear me come in. I stood in the kitchen and listened, a feat I'd honed to perfection by that age. Grandma's sweet, raspy voice floated to me. "She's a sweet child, but Darcy's the pretty one."

Papa's voice was lower and harder to hear, but I caught every word. "It's a shame she don't favor her mama. She might'a had a chance in this world."

Something hurt deep down inside, like a stream of water that started at my throat and ran down my insides to my stomach and plunked there like a rock. I figured this was what Daddy meant when he said that things were sometimes hard to swallow. This was hard.

I'd always believed that Grandma loved me. I'd never known for sure about Papa, though Mama said he'd loved me more than all the other grandchildren when I was a baby. But I couldn't remember that. All I could remember was how he never said anything to anybody, just grunted and sucked on his pipe. I didn't think he knew anything, so it didn't bother me. But Grandma saying it sure did.

I slipped out so Grandma and Papa wouldn't know I'd been there. I decided not to like either of them anymore. I was not going to let it hurt me. My motto was, "Sticks and stones may break my bones but words …". All of a sudden, the thought came to me. Did Sam stick his teeth out at me because he didn't like me and thought I was ugly?

I couldn't eat dinner that night. I didn't say a word. Even when Mattie asked me questions, I just shook my head yes or no. Beth said I was acting foolish, but I had no idea what she meant and, frankly, didn't care in the least what she thought. She was a pest anyhow. Ben was scowling as usual, and I didn't care about him, either. It was Sam I was wondering about. A couple of times I glanced at him, but his teeth stayed in his mouth. He wasn't even looking at me. "Oh, my God," I thought. "I'm so ugly he can't even look at me no more." With that, I ran from the table squalling, "I can't help it 'cause I'm ugly. I didn't ask to be born."

I wanted to go home. Mama and Daddy never said mean things like that about me, so I figured they must love me as I was. Daddy had never, ever stuck his teeth out at me. Mattie tried to find out why I was so upset but I wouldn't talk about it. I couldn't; it was too humiliating. I walked outside to think about what they had said and try to get it straight in my mind.

Ben came out. "Jessie, I'm sorry I hurt your feelings. I ain't never had nothing against you. You're all right."

He shoved me good-naturedly, but I slapped his shoulder and chest and called him names. He looked at the ground and walked away. I half-way felt sorry for him, then decided not to. He deserved it, being hateful to me all summer.

All of a sudden, I missed my mama. She was my soft world when I was hurt or sad or afraid, and right now I was all three. I went inside, stood very straight in front of Sam and Mattie. I explained to them how I wanted them to call Mama and Daddy to come get me. I was tired of staying in such a place; I no longer wanted to stay where I was made fun of, now do it right away. I made sure to stare at the spaces between their eyes and not directly into them so they couldn't tell what I was thinking.

Sam stared back at me. Then he spoke. "Jessie, I'll call if you want. But first, you gotta tell me what's got your goat so bad. Ain't gonna be no call till you do."

He wasn't kidding, and I knew that he wasn't, but I was not going to tell them I'd heard my own grandparents saying I was ugly. First of all, it was bad to listen in on other people's conversations and second, it was awful to admit to people that I knew I was ugly. They'd probably agree, and that would be even more horrible. I shook my head no. Then I walked to the bedroom, closed the door, and fell across the bed. I let the sobs come up from my stomach and settle in the mattress in long, low groans.

The next day, Mattie didn't ask me to get James for breakfast. He was in the house when I got up, and the food was already on the table. We ate without saying a word, and when everybody finished eating, we all got up and left. The quiet was eerie. I went to the front porch to sit on the glider and feel sorry for myself. Sadie was tending the mums and gladiolus that Mattie set out in clay pots every spring. She didn't look at me, but I could tell she had her mind set on me.

"Sweet child, you've done gone and upset everybody here, you know that?" She kept her back to me, continuing her watering. I nodded, knowing she wasn't looking at me.

"Girl, ain't no reason in this here world for you to go and do that. Can't just keep on doing this, now."

Tears suddenly popped out of my eyes, and I couldn't hold back. "Sadie, I heard Grandma and Papa talking and saying I was ugly." There! I'd said it.

She stopped watering and turned to me. Her face lit up. Then her mouth stretched across her face in a wide grin. "Is that all that's going on with you?" She plopped her fists on her hips.

"Is that all?" I was appalled at her attitude. "Is that all? That's a bad thing my own grandparents have done said about me. They don't love me."

She cocked her head, and her face turned soft and loving. "Oh, my sweet Jessie, you ain't ugly. You got a face like them models up in New Yawk. It's just your Grandma and Papa, they ain't never seen such beauty as is here before my eyes, and they just don't know how to treat it." She sounded as if she meant it.

"I ain't pretty like that. I'm skinny, and my eyes are too big, and so's my mouth. My hair's too black for a white girl and too straight, and my nose is big like Daddy's. It's awful to be so ugly, Sadie. Only I wish nobody'd told me I was bad ugly." With that, I broke down in sobs.

Sadie gathered me in her arms. "Jessie, you the most precious girl that ever was seen. You got that something that makes people love to be around you. You wait till you grow up and watch how people hang around you and loves you."

Maybe I had to believe her, or die thinking I was the ugliest person there ever was, but I suddenly found myself considering her words. "If I'm not ugly, then how come it is Sam sticks his teeth out at me?"

"Honey child, if Sam don't like nobody he don't stick his teeth out. He sticks 'em out because he do like you. I know it don't make no sense, but that's the way it is in this old world. People likes you, they stick they teeth out at you. They don't like you; they just go on 'bout they business and don't pay you no never mind."

My heart felt the sunshine. Maybe Sadie was right. Maybe Sam didn't think I was so ugly he couldn't stand to look at me. As she always had, she'd managed to heal my heart. I hugged her tight and skipped inside.

"Sam! Mattie! I've been talking with Sadie, and I'm better now."

Just as I bounded through the door, I came face to face with Sam. He looked down at me and grinned. Before I could take a breath, his teeth jumped out, this time chattering as if they were going to eat me where I stood. I screamed with laughter and took off running.

"Mattie! Sam done stuck his teeth out at me again."

Sadie's sweet humming floated in from the porch.

Monkey Seeds

Sometimes, after supper, while we would be watching television, Daddy would suddenly slap the arms of his rust recliner and say, "I think I'm gonna make some peanut brittle." He would flash his gap-toothed grin and head toward Mama's clean kitchen. Bobby and I would be up and off the settee and in the kitchen, hunting for pans, before Mama had time to frown and push her glasses up.

Of course, we knew she would whine about how Daddy was going to mess up her kitchen, and she'd have to work her fingers to the bone to get it cleaned up. And she was tired after working and slaving over a hot stove all day. But we didn't much care about all that. Peanut brittle was fun to make and good to eat. We loved peanut brittle.

Daddy made the best there was in the whole wide world, we knew that for certain. Darcy, being older and developed by now, or so Grandma said when I hid behind the settee listening to grownups talk, pretended great lack of interest in what we were doing. She would yawn and stretch her freckled arms out in front of her, wiggle her behind to the front of the chair so she would have a good reason to stand up.

Before you know it, though, she'd be in the kitchen with us singing "You are my sunshine" and hoping to make

Mama happy even if there was going to be a mess and she was going to have to clean it up by herself. Sometimes, it worked. Other times, it didn't work. This night, it did not.

Mama had canned a cabinet full of peaches and left the peach seeds on the counter for Daddy to take to his workshop. There, he would carve them into little monkeys. Well, Bobby grabbed a seed and threw it at me. I never was one not to take a dare, so I felt the need to throw one back at him, even though I didn't actually hear the dare. I popped one back. Darcy got hit and screamed like she was dying, and I got in trouble when Bobby started it.

I tell you right now, I was darn mad about being the only one blamed for the whole thing. Bobby was such a snit. I learned that word from my aunt when she was mad at me, so I figured it must be pretty bad. Besides, she wasn't the only one in this family who knew big words.

We watched Daddy make the brittle and pour it from one dish to another, quickly so it wouldn't set up too fast. After we had eaten until we could eat no more, we had to go to bed, leaving Mama alone in the kitchen, cleaning up and mumbling how she hated peanut brittle and peach seeds anyway. Daddy was humming some railroad song as he carried the seeds out to his building. We knew he'd be out there until morning and Mama would be mad and pouting at him all day, but we didn't care because we were full of peanut brittle.

The morning was about what we expected. Mama slammed biscuits and gravy on the table like we were the enemy. We knew it was because of Daddy, but none of us had the nerve to say anything to her when she was like this. I take that back. Darcy usually had the nerve, but she always got in trouble when she did. Bobby and I watched whatever happened to her and, if it was awful, we didn't do it.

"I like this biscuit, Mama."

I smiled the sweetest, the most loving smile I could muster at her, hoping the frown would go away. It didn't do any good. She sat down, put her elbow on the yellow-topped table and picked at her food.

"Mama, I got a test today."

Darcy raised her eyebrows at Mama as if she needed an answer to a question, but even I knew she hadn't asked a question. Honestly, Darcy could be so dumb sometimes. When she didn't get a response from Mama, she lowered her head and seemed to pout.

I went about my biscuit and gravy eating with a vengeance. Bobby sat the way he always did. I wasn't a chicken like him, just wise enough to know when to be quiet.

Daddy came in the back door, and he wasn't humming. He looked horrible and smelled worse. I hated it when he reeked like that. I'd sniffed the whiskey he kept in the building, and sometimes in the truck, but it was never as bad as the way he smelled after drinking it.

"Daddy, you smell like something the cat drug in." I scrunched my nose and put my hand over it.

He looked at me as if I had hit him and he was going to hit me back. "What'd you say?"

I smiled. "I said you smell something awful, and I thank it's a good smell." I lied.

What would you expect a girl to do if her life was in danger because she was too honest? Lying was important in my life, and I'd worked it out so that I was good at it by then. It had saved my neck a few times already. I kept smiling at him until he grinned at me, showing that space again. I hated the space but there wasn't anything I could do about it, so I tried not to look at it.

Mama kept her elbow on the table and wouldn't look at Daddy. She was still mad at him, either for the peanut brittle, or the peach seeds he kept whittling away at, or maybe for the drinking that he did in the building. Mama never went to his building when he was out there. She'd stay in the house and pout. I guess she was mad about the drinking, even though she started being mad when he decided to make the peanut brittle.

Daddy slouched over to her and leaned down to kiss her. She turned her face away so that his kiss landed on her cheek, which is what she normally did, and he'd pretend not to notice.

"Here you go, sweetheart. A monkey just to say I love you."

He laid a peach seed monkey on the table next to her plate and shuffled to the bedroom. We heard him groan when he landed on the bed and knew he'd be out the rest of the day. He wouldn't even hear us if got into fights and screamed at each other.

Mama always said that he was dead to the world, and it appeared that he was. She knew him, too, so we paid close attention to what she said most of the time. How were we supposed to pay much attention to what Daddy said? He was drunk about as often as he was sober, and drunk talk didn't mean what it said. We knew that much if nothing else.

I figured I had two daddies, one sober and one drunk. The drunk one wasn't too useful in decision-making plans, but the sober one protected us and took care of us. He was crucial to our plans. It worked out well that way for me. I don't know how Darcy and Bobby worked their confusions out. It was hard enough keeping my own thoughts straight; I sure couldn't worry about theirs.

Mama started crying, and Darcy and Bobby left the table. I don't know why they did that. They just did. I guess they didn't know what to say when she cried. I did, though. I went around the table and stood beside her, patting the hand that held the monkey.

"It's all right, Mama. Daddy don't mean to be bad; he's just that way, and I guess he can't help it."

I looked at the monkey in her hand and started laughing. Mama looked at me, eyes all wet around them and her nose running a little bit. She wiped it with the dishrag.

"What you laughing at?" She seemed defensive as if she thought I was laughing at her. I wouldn't even be caught dead laughing at my mama.

"I'm laughing at that monkey. Ain't it cute?"

She turned it over and nodded. It got funnier and funnier looking to me. "Look, it's biting its tail, Mama." I laughed harder, but Mama just shook her head.

"That's what monkeys do, Jessie. They bite their tails. I don't know why, though."

"I'm glad we don't have to bite our tails like that." I knew I'd made a funny before I even got the whole thing out of my mouth.

A smile started on Mama's mouth, grew wider and wider as she gazed at the monkey. I'd gotten through to her and knew what would happen next. She'd start laughing at the monkey, then say it was cute because my daddy made it and I should be ashamed of myself, laughing at something he made, so go to my room and stay there.

Later, I'd hear her talking sweetly to Daddy in their room, and I could go to sleep unafraid somebody was going to throw something at someone and wake me up so that my heart would jump too much. I hated waking up like that.

Sometimes, I'd have to hold my heart to keep it from jumping too big and popping right on out of me. You had to be pretty smart to stay ahead of these people, but I could do it better than Darcy and Bobby. Darcy fussed at them, and that didn't do any good. Bobby hid from them, and that sure didn't help.

When everybody was asleep, I tiptoed into the kitchen to steal some peanut brittle. I slid down the wall next to the stove so I couldn't be seen while I ate it, trying not to crunch and wake anybody up. Everything was so quiet it made the crunching seem loud as an airplane, but I kept eating until I saw something on the floor next to the sink.

I scooted on my bottom across the floor to find out what it was. It was one of Daddy's little peach seed monkeys. I carried it back to my peanut brittle eating place and turned it over in my hand, giving it a good once over. It looked exactly like a monkey, with two tiny eyes on either side of its head. There were little legs and arms, and a monkey-like face. Its arms were attached to a long tail which went to his mouth, and it made him look like he was biting his tail. Then I looked closer and saw a teeny piece of peanut brittle sticking out of its mouth, and it scared me half to death.

I threw the monkey across the room as if it were some kind of monster about to eat me alive. As far as I knew, it planned to. I mean, how many peach seeds do you see that can eat peanut brittle? This required the cavalry, and I didn't care that the cavalry needed its sleep. I needed reinforcements more than they could possibly need sleep. I ran down the hall to their bedroom and burst through the door screaming.

"Mama! Daddy! You gotta come to the kitchen!"

With that loud battle cry, I spun on one foot and headed back to the kitchen and the brittle-eating peach seed monkey, Mama, and Daddy on my heels, Daddy in his underwear and Mama in a flowered nightgown trying to hide her bosoms.

"Jessie, I declare! What's the matter with you?"

Mama was always wondering what was wrong with me, but I could never tell her because I didn't know myself. Daddy, as usual, kept quiet until he could figure out the right thing to say. They stood in the middle of the kitchen staring at me. I pointed to the monkey on the floor.

"Look! It's eating peanut brittle. It's alive!" I thought about crying but decided that might be a little too over the top, so I took deep, panting breaths to prove how frightened I was.

Daddy picked the monkey up and turned it around in his hand, frowning as if I'd lost my mind and Mama started frowning and put her hands on her hips. That meant I'd just about pushed her past her pushing place.

Daddy grinned. "It's just the monkey I give your mama. That's all." Then he looked kind of sad that I'd found it on the floor, and glanced at Mama. She ignored him.

"But it's eating peanut brittle, Daddy. How can it eat things? It ain't supposed to be able to eat things."

He threw his head back and guffawed. Now, that about made me mad. I didn't like people making fun of me, especially when I was being serious and was genuinely scared, not make believing.

"I put peanut brittle in its mouth. I thought it'd be cute, for your mama."

I felt stupid. I did not like feeling stupid, either. Putting my hands on my hips, I stuck one foot out to the side in a serious manner. "Well, I knew that. I just thought I'd scare ya'll."

I knew they knew I was lying, but all of us pretended I wasn't so we could all go back to bed. Mama saw the peanut brittle crumbs next to the stove and sent me to bed saying she would take care of my smartness in the morning, but right now they needed sleep.

I tried to sleep, but my eyes stayed open. Daddy sometimes had a habit of not telling the truth, so how was I to know if he was telling the truth now. Besides, if he gave the monkey to Mama, how did it get on the floor next to the sink? Then I remembered. I'd seen Mama open the cabinet door and toss the monkey toward the trash can. It had hurt my heart because I knew Daddy had made it just for her, to say he was sorry. She hadn't cared if he was sorry or not. I guess it must have missed the trash can and landed on the floor without either of us noticing.

I decided, though, to watch more carefully the next time Daddy made one of his peach seed monkeys, which is what he did just about every time he drank too much in the summer. He could get a lot of seeds because peaches grew in the summer. I didn't think I'd care too much about eating any more peanut brittle. It seemed to make Mama unhappy every time Daddy made it, and he did weird things every time, also.

I sure didn't want to see any more seeds acting like they were coming to life. It was hard enough trying to keep this family sane on a daily basis. I certainly didn't want to have to keep them alive. That was a bit too much for a girl my age.to a house with cracks in the floor.

Olive

"It ain't right, people owning other people."

"*Poor* Olive; it must be awful for her knowing her great granddaddy was owned by your daddy's granddaddy."

Daddy told Mama to shut her mouth; she didn't know what in the hell she was talking about, and anyway, that's the way it was in Morgan in them days. Somebody had to pick the damn cotton.

I had no idea what they were talking about and sure didn't want to be yelled at like that, so I kept quiet. That was the way I lived my life: scrunched in a corner or behind a couch, listening to grownups work out problems and gossip to each other. I learned a lot that way, even what they thought about me. That way, I could like them or not like them, and they'd never know why.

Where Olive was concerned, all that mattered to me was that we were friends. She and I had a secret spot in the woods between our houses where we could go and play. It was a batch of honeysuckle where we could squat in the vines and suck the juice from the yellow flowers, talk about the different ways our folks did things, and dream. We loved it. Mama said we shouldn't be friends, that it wasn't proper. She said people wouldn't understand. Some said it wasn't right to have friends like Olive, but I didn't know why. Because I didn't know why, I ignored them and skipped down the road to meet her whenever I wanted, or could get away without getting caught.

Olive's mama didn't care if we played together or not. She even made cookies for us to eat when we were at our playhouse pretending to be mothers to our dolls. We sometimes forced Cato, Olive's little brother, to be the daddy, but we made him work too hard at being a good one instead of a mean one, so he didn't often want to play with us.

Now and again, these many years past, when I happen upon a child's enormous eyes gazing up at me with that diligent search for answers to questions that I have no answer to, I remember Olive. That's when I wish I had known her last name, or where she moved when she left Morgan. Or where she might be now. It's then that I recall years of fierceness and violence, years of hate that ate at lives instead of allowing children to play in honeysuckle with secret friends.

Daddy often came home late smelling like whiskey. When he did, he hurled the dishes through the house and jerked the tablecloth off the table. It was on those nights that I'd sneak out my window and run to Olive's house. Her folks left the doors open so they wouldn't suffocate in the heat, so

I never had a problem getting inside where I'd squat on the floor next to her bed and wet my panties. It happened every time, but nobody made me feel bad about it.

Olive's house had cracks in the floor that we would peek through to watch the mice run around. Sometimes, we'd tie cheese to strings and hang them through the cracks to feed the mice. We figured they had to get hungry always hiding under there. Mama said that having mice was wrong, but they were so cute trying to get the cheese from the string, I forgot her warning about them bringing diseases. I couldn't see that they brought anything. Those hard years were good years, though, because of Olive and her family. That is, until life, as it really was, cut in on us.

We were sucking flowers and pretending I was the lady with the cotton plantation and Olive was my maid one day, when she suddenly stuck her hip out, planted her fist on it, and yelled she was going to be the plantation lady, and I had to be her maid for a change. Well! That would not do at all.

"That ain't real life, Olive. We're playing real life, not pretend. You gotta be the maid, and I gotta be the rich lady."

"I ain't gotta be nobody's maid no more."

She shoved me into the honeysuckle and mice scampered over me, leaving their dirty feet prints all over my flowered dress. I knew that I would die from diseases if they didn't get off me. By the time we'd stopped fighting, and I'd managed to free myself, my face red from heat and anger, I no longer wanted Olive as my friend.

She said, "I don't care," and we went our separate ways, now and again looking over our shoulders to see what the other was doing. I wanted to turn around and tell her I was sorry for something, but I didn't know what I should be sorry for.

When I slammed into the house, Mama's mouth dropped a foot. "What in the world happened to you? Your dress is filthy."

"Olive. She pushed me down, and I got the disease from mice. I hate her, and I don't want to play with her again. She's just mean as a snake."

"I told you not to play with that girl, Jessie. They ain't like us."

She settled a clenched fist on her hips. I didn't like it when she posed that way. It made me feel unimportant and reminded me of the way Olive stood before she pushed me.

"She ain't different from us. We act just the same and think the same. She's just mean; that's all."

Mama glared at me. "Jessie Mae, you're the most frustrating youngun I ever saw. You don't listen to a thing I say. I told you and told you, at least a million times, to leave that little black girl alone. It ain't right to play with folks like that. Can't nothing but bad come from it."

"It don't make sense, though, Mama. How come friends have to be the same color? I ain't never seen nobody that's white. So how can I have white friends? Huh? Tell me that, hateful."

I was serious. My mama was, too. Slapped my mouth before I saw it coming.

"Shame on you, young lady. You ought to have the daylight beat out of you for saying such things and calling me names."

"Well, ain't nobody I know of that's white. Daddy's red, and you got pink on you; Darcy's got brown dots everywhere. Bobby's tan." I closed my eyes for a second slap, but nothing happened. She turned around and walked away. My mouth felt fat and hot.

For weeks I pined for Olive. When Mama told Daddy that she had pushed me down and got my dress dirty, he stomped out of the house and down the road and incinerated our home with his cigarette lighter. I cried until I threw up. I pleaded with him not to murder the animals, but he told me to hush my whining and get my butt back to the house, or he'd beat the tar out of me. I went home, sulked for days, and hoped he'd feel guilty for burning up all that honeysuckle.

It was a long time before I saw Olive again. I was downtown with Mama, and Olive was across the street with her mama. White folks stayed on the one side of the street in those days, and Olive's people stayed on the other, except on Saturdays when the whites stayed home and let them have the town. I didn't understand why they did things like that but also knew enough about what was going on not to ask too many questions.

We watched each other, but we didn't smile. Something inside me ached, though, like a toothache throbs. I didn't know what to do about it since the whole thing was Olive's fault: hitting me and getting my dress dirty. If it hadn't been for her, Daddy wouldn't have burned the honeysuckle. It was her fault, too, that the animals lost their homes or had to move. I wouldn't consider that they might have died. I wouldn't speak to her, and she deserved it. But I was still sad.

One night, Daddy smelled like whiskey when he came home, and I started to climb out the window to go to Olive's house. Then I remembered I didn't have a friend anymore and smashed my pillow over my head so they couldn't hear me. I cried, furious with Olive all over again. Here I was, afraid and needing my friend, and she'd messed it all up. That's when I decided that I would never have a friend that did not exactly match me. Mama was right. Olive didn't appreciate me, even turned on me, wanting to be the southern lady and take away my rights. Daddy always said we had rights and nobody should try to take them away from us. Now I understood what he meant. Everybody knew the lady had to be white and her maid had to be like Olive. That's the way it was, even if it didn't make a lick of sense to anybody. But I was still unhappy, and I still missed my friend.

A year later, while taking a walk with my dog, I came to the honeysuckle patch where Olive and I used to play. My heart felt like it bloomed right there. I could not believe my eyes. Honeysuckle grew everywhere, bigger and fluffier than it had been before. I decided God had remade it so the critters could have warm, sweet smelling homes and not have to wander around searching for them.

I leaped into the vines and rolled with the mice, not caring at all about my dress. Buddy bounced with me, yapping and chasing lizards. It was wonderful to be happy again. Then, I remembered Olive. At that point, I didn't care that she had pushed me down. I had a fleeting thought that it could have even been my fault. After all, I wouldn't let her be the lady, and it would be awful if you always had to be the maid.

I scrambled from the vines, my heart pounding so hard I could hear it in my ears. Olive would be so happy to see me and to learn that she could be the wealthy lady at long last. I rounded the curve and stopped. I could not get my bearings. My brain whirled chaotically as if it were lost and unable to work. Olive's house had burned to the ground. Nothing was left except a little bit of cinder block, a chimney standing by itself, and black charred wood. I screamed her name and ran, praying that she would answer me. But she didn't answer. Olive was gone.

Mama said that Olive's house had burned months back, and they had moved away, but she didn't know where. It wasn't our business, anyhow. "They weren't like us."

I couldn't sleep for thinking about Olive, reliving how I'd refused to be her friend the right way for so long. God took her away and now I was too late. I tried to cry in my pillow so no one would hear, but Darcy heard and slapped me because I bothered her. Even Darcy couldn't rile me, though. I was too furious with myself to be angry at her. My only friend was gone. There would never be another friend as perfect as Olive, not for me. And all because my people used to own her people, and I wouldn't let her get out of being owned.

One day, as I was playing "Doodle Bug, Doodle Bug" beneath the living room window, open on account of the heat, I heard my mama and daddy talking. They were deciding which bills to pay this month and which ones to put off until next month, fussing about which one spent too much money. Mama fussed at Daddy about how mean he was to people.

"You were even mean to Jessie, doing what you did to her little friend; even if they ain't like us, they ought to be treated decently."

I couldn't think of a friend my daddy had been mean to. The only one I ever had was Olive, and I didn't have her anymore.

"I don't want no sass from you, woman."

Mama snapped back. "I ought to tell Jessie what you did to Olive's house."

Daddy jumped up from his chair, and I shut my eyes and covered my ears. I figured he would hit her for being smart mouthed, but he didn't. He just stood over her, threatening to beat the hell out of her if she didn't shut her damn mouth.

Mama kept on, though. "It wasn't bad enough you had to burn up their honeysuckle home, so they didn't have a place to play. Oh, no! You had to go and burn down that child's house."

I heard her, but it didn't make sense. How could Daddy burn down a house? I shook my head to get the words out of my brain, but they stayed there: static, cooked in. Carved.

Daddy stomped to the kitchen, mumbling they deserved it; he'd do it again if he had half a chance. Mama had told the truth! My own daddy had burned down my friend's house. My own daddy! Why would a daddy do such a thing? I could stand it no longer, stood up and peered through the window screen.

"Daddy! You burn down Olive's house?"

Shock kept my eyes too wide open, and my heart pounded way too fast. At first, it felt as if I might pass out and die, but fear of getting stiff and hard, the way dead people get, scared me more than Daddy did, so I kept breathing. Daddy whirled toward the window, fist in mid-air ready to hit me. He couldn't, though, because I was outside and the screen protected me.

"You ain't supposed to be hiding out there listening in on people's talks. Get yourself in here right now, young lady."

I went inside and stood in front him, staring straight into his eyes. I had a way of staring people down and making them give in if I worked at it hard enough. Daddy didn't give in to my way, though. He turned me across his knee and thrashed me with my own hairbrush, and then ordered me to get to my room and stay there until he said I could come out.

Mama nagged. "She didn't do anything wrong. You're the mean one, burning up houses just because you don't like somebody. Next thing you know, you'll be burning ours down."

It was a bad night. Mama got in as much trouble as I did, and neither one of us felt we'd done anything wrong. I thought about it all night, wondering how he did it, and why he did it, and what happened to Olive and her brothers and sisters. And who would I go to see when fear jumped up and grabbed me in the night.

The morning was no better. Mama had a swollen nose and pouted with Daddy. He was still mad at me. I already knew he was mean, but a person has to be meaner than a snake to burn down houses. I ate without saying anything as long as I could, then dropped my fork and glared.

"How come you burn down Olive's house?" I stuck my chin up to show how serious I was.

He didn't even bother to look at me, just kept slurping his food and making those horrible smacking noises that I hated, then left the table. I followed, knowing I was treading on dangerous ground.

"It was my fault, Daddy. It weren't Olive's."

"Don't matter. There's right, and there's wrong, and hitting my kid's wrong. Lest I do it."

That was it. No more explanations. I knew to stop asking questions. When I looked at Mama, hands outstretched for help, she shrugged. I thought my heart would break. I thought about the agony Olive, and her family must have suffered watching their home burn to the ground. What happened to the dogs and cats that slept inside? Had they burned, too?

I couldn't sleep that night, so I eased out of bed and tiptoed into their room, put my hand on Mama's shoulder and shook her. "Mama, I need to talk to you," I whispered so I wouldn't wake Daddy.

She shushed me with a slender finger to her lips and slipped out of bed and went to the kitchen, where she put on a pot of coffee so we could talk. Mama couldn't do anything without coffee. She loved it. I decided to learn to love it, too, to be like my mama, the only good in life I knew.

"I can't go on living knowing my friend might need me." My chin quivered, but I worked hard not to cry.

"She'll be all right, Jessie. She's got a mama and daddy that'll take care of her. Ain't no need of you going on so; nothing you can do about it anyhow."

"But I need to make it up to her. I ain't mad at her anymore and I need to tell that I ain't. She needs to be the lady of the plantation house."

"What on earth are you talking about?"

"When we played plantation, she had to be the maid so I could be the lady, and she wanted to swap places for a change. I didn't let her and she got mad, and that's why she pushed me down. It was my fault. She needs to find out what it's like to be the rich lady for once."

"She'll find out someday, hon."

"No, she won't, neither, Mama. People won't ever let her. They ain't kind to Olive, and I don't know why they ain't. Please help me find out where they moved."

She looked at me and smiled a tender smile. When she did that, the whole world lit up. It was like the sun popped up before the dark was gone. I knew that Mama felt, deep down, the same way I did about Olive and her family and that she would end up helping me find them. Nobody else would, though. I didn't dare let Daddy know. He didn't like her being my friend in the first place, and now he'd done a horrible thing, and I almost hated him for it. I needed to find her and tell her that I loved her and wanted to be her maid. I needed to do that. Mama agreed to ask around the next day.

"Maybe somebody will know where they went. I'm sorry your daddy don't understand, Jessie, but I understand. I hope that makes it a little better."

"It does, Mama."

"I had a friend once like Olive, and my daddy didn't want us being friends, either. We slipped around so nobody would know."

A far-away look visited in her eyes, and I knew that she was thinking about that friend. I wondered who her friend had been and where she had gone but also knew to let it be. If she wanted me to know, she would tell me. That's the way she was. I wanted to hug her but remembered that our family did not hug. Olive's family did, though. They even hugged me. That's how I knew how it felt to be held close for good reasons.

A couple of weeks later, Mama came home from the grocery store and called for me. "Jessie, come in and help me put the groceries away."

I could tell by the sound of her voice that she had good news, and was pretending she needed help. Darcy and Daddy didn't hear those sounds in her voice, though, because I was the only one who could hear sounds that were not in words. Sometimes, I could tell what people were thinking by how they said their words, or by how they looked at me. It was fun: reading minds. I ran in, slid halfway across the kitchen floor before stopping.

"You find out something?" I stood stiffly, waiting.

"Where's your daddy and them?"

"Outside."

"Down the Parker Road about two miles. They have a better house over there, so your daddy messed up bad if he was trying to hurt them."

I could have flown like a bird down Parker Road to Olive's house, but had to wait until after supper when Daddy went to work on shift. Mama could settle down and sew our clothes, and I could ride Darcy's bike down there.

It was so hard, waiting was. I waved at Daddy as he drove off, then headed down the road, singing songs Olive had taught me when I would run to her house on nights I was afraid.

Mama told the truth. Their new house was nicer than the other one. It had real glass in the windows and a door that closed all the way. I wondered if there were cracks in the floor. If not, I bet Olive felt sad about not being able to feed the mice.

I rode into the clean-swept yard and vaulted off the bike while it rolled, hollering Olive's name. Cato came out, curious about what I wanted. He looked angry, and it made me nervous.

"Hey, Cato! I need to see Olive!"

He ran into the house and left me standing there. Olive came out and stood on the porch, arms folded in front of her. "What you want?"

"Hey, Olive." I tried to smile, but my lips wouldn't work right.

"Don't give me none of your grinning, girl. I said, what you want?"

"I just come to say I'm sorry."

"Yeah? What you sorry for?"

"I'm sorry for what my daddy did. He was real bad to do that, and I'm sorry he did. I told him I was mad at him for it."

"What else you sorry for?" Her arms relaxed.

"I'm sorry I wouldn't let you be the rich lady."

"I don't want to be her."

"Well, I want to be your maid."

She just stood there, staring at me. My heart pounded. I thought she might be able to hear it.

"Olive, I love you, and I don't want another friend but you. Please, let's forgive and forget."

I'd heard Mama say that people had to forgive and forget, and let sleeping dogs lay. I didn't know about sleeping dogs, but I did understand what forgive and forget meant. I wanted Olive to forgive me and forget the bad things I did to her. Especially what my daddy did.

"I guess I love you, too, girl." A smile spread across her face.

I dropped the bike and ran. We hugged and giggled, then went inside where Olive's mother had been watching through the window. She opened her arms, and I melted into them. It was so wonderful to be back with Olive and her family. I looked at her mama.

"My mama said she used to have a friend like Olive when she was a little girl."

She nodded and turned toward the kitchen. "I guess you girls want some milk and cookies to take to that honeysuckle patch that done grown up all over the road."

Cato ran in yelling that somebody was in the yard asking for his mama. Olive's mother glanced outside the window; her face turned pale.

"Well, I'll be …" she whispered to herself as she pushed open the door.

"Lawsy, girl! What in the world you doing here?"

The screen door slammed behind Olive's mama, and a sweet voice floated to us.

"I missed my old friend."

Arm in arm, Olive and I joined our mothers on the porch.

One Potato

"One potato, two potatoes, three potatoes, four …

five potatoes, six potatoes, seven potatoes, more!"

"*You're* out, Jessie." I despised that stupid game and was always the first to sit out. Deciding there must be a trick to it, I determined to learn the trick and be the winner for a change. But Mama said it wasn't a trick, it was just that I didn't like to lose. She was probably right; usually was. I loved my mama, but sometimes she was frustrating.

And so was my disposition on that day. Hot and sweaty from running and not liking the cousins I found myself forced to play with on this visit to Granny's house, when they called me out, rage that hung around me like a cloud erupted.

"I ain't out! Ya'll are stupid, and I don't wanna play no more."

I stomped away, heading for the plank swing hanging from the oak behind the house. I told myself that I would play alone and enjoy the day. My own presence was far better than being with any of them. Swinging was a delight anyway. Hanging backward, letting my straight hair drag the ground, looking upside down at grownups sitting around and jabbering was invigorating. It made the world look nice, too, without all the mean glares and hateful words that floated around and through me when I was standing straight.

The women sat on the porch rocking and fanning, some of them with baby blankets over their shoulders nursing kids, some fussing about the men at the picnic table who talked about deer hunting the night before and who shot what and how good a shot he was. I hated night hunting. Mostly, because I had to go and help kill the deer and then I couldn't sleep for nights on end for seeing those poor things drop where they stood.

The men drove around until they saw a deer, then they made us kids hold a flashlight and shine it in his eyes so he would stop and stare at the lights. Then they shot him. I would slap my hands over my eyes to keep from seeing the poor thing fall. It was a grisly sight. Daddy said I didn't know what in the hell I was talking about for saying it was unfair, the deer needed a fighting chance, and he said, "You'd better not have ruined that flashlight when you dropped it in the dirt."

"Jessie's a crybaby." Bobby annoyed me as usual, but I kept swinging, hoping he'd get near enough for me to kick out and knock him flat.

Having a brother like Bobby was hard on a girl, what with his continual poking and picking, and Mama wouldn't let me beat the devil out of him, which made it tougher to be around him. When she wasn't looking, though, I'd drag him off the settee and try to make his head hit the floor. He never did get hurt because he'd grab his head and protect it, but coming close to causing him pain was worth the thrashing I'd get for doing it.

"Shut up, Bobby. You don't even know what a crybaby is."

I stopped swinging and sat up, enjoying the way my brain felt while it settled from being in the wrong place.

"Hey, Jessie! Wanna shoot the B.B. gun?"

My feet were running before I slung myself from the swing and hit the ground. John William knew what I liked and was always coming to my rescue in times like these. I could shoot like Annie Oakley. My daddy taught us all how to shoot with his twenty-two. Sometimes Aunt Corrie would line up garbage cans and let us shoot at them. I generally won, too, so the cousins didn't much like to play it with me. John William didn't mind losing to me, though.

"Get the guns, John William. Hot diggity!" I was happy.

Aunt Corrie lined the cans up while we tossed the bat to see who would go first and I won. I could hardly believe it. I raised the gun, cocked it and shot before she'd had time to say "one for your money." Everybody heard her scream, and I closed my eyes. I knew she had to be bleeding by the way she shrieked, and I hated to see blood.

I thought to myself, "I hope she ain't gonna die."

When the screeching stopped, I opened my eyes. Aunt Corrie was holding her chubby arm and moaning. The other adults were gathering around her like bees at a hive. Cousins had deserted me. Even John William. They'd scattered so far nobody knew where they went until everything was over and they started peeking out of hiding places.

I swallowed. I'd gone and done it up good this time, and I knew it. This was bad. I figured a walloping was the least of my worries. When I heard Daddy's voice, I knew I was a dead duck. Everything was so quiet I could feel the hairs on the back of my neck get stiff and stand up like soldiers at attention.

"Jessie, get your tail over here."

"Yes, sir."

Everybody said I had a beautiful smile, and a magnificent one was needed at this point, so I put a smile on my face that should have charmed a prince. Letting the gun slide from my hand, I sauntered over to Daddy, standing near enough to hear him but far enough away to keep from getting backhanded. His twinkling eyes were not twinkling. They were dead set on me. I felt like a deer in headlights. His eyes looked black. It felt as if my heart was going to beat on out of my body and run away like a coward.

That thought—running away—crossed my mind but flitted on through because I didn't have anywhere to go that I wouldn't have to come back sooner or later. This whole thing had to be faced square on like Daddy always said, "You got to go on out there and meet life head on." I was about to confront it dead on.

"Look at what you did. You shot your Aunt Corrie. What you got to say for yourself?" He waited. I smiled. "I ain't wanting none of your grinning, Jessie Mae. Get that smirk off your face."

My mind would not think. Most of the time I imagined stories quickly. Not this time. I didn't know why I'd done it myself; how was I supposed to explain it to anybody else? Then I had an idea. I'd cry. I contorted my face and tried to push tears out of my eyes, knowing with everything in me that he'd feel sorry for me. I thought wrong.

"Don't give me no pretend crying. You done shot your aunt and ain't no reason for it. Look at her."

Daddy was not like Mama; he paid little attention to my acting abilities. I had to look at Aunt Corrie but feared I'd die if I saw blood. When I glanced at her, she cast a radiant smile my way. Her being nice when I'd done such a dastardly deed to her did me in, and I started crying in earnest.

"I didn't mean to do it. It was by accident."

She came to me and hugged me. "Jessie didn't mean to shoot. I think the gun went off on its own, didn't it, sweetheart?" She winked at me.

Suddenly, I couldn't lie any longer. "No, ma'am. I didn't wait like you said to do because I didn't want to lose. I didn't want to get you shot, though."

There I was, telling the truth. This was not the girl I'd known all my life. I reasoned that I must really like Aunt Corrie to feel so rotten about shooting her, and for sure to tell the truth about it. I half-way wished I hadn't been a bad sport playing "Potato." If I'd been a good sport, John William wouldn't have suggested the guns, and I wouldn't have shot her and been standing here facing execution. The fleeting thought of blaming John William passed through my brain and scooted on out because he was too good for me to give him any fault for my mean ways.

Daddy tried to dig the pellet from Aunt Corrie's arm with his pocket knife, but it slid around so he couldn't make it pop out. She gritted her teeth and made funny squeaking noises while he dug but finally said she couldn't take it anymore so he stopped. He never did get it out. She walked around for good with a little blue dot on her arm.

My punishment was worse than I imagined it would be. I had to peel potatoes for supper. Granny said for me to use the peeler and not the paring knife so I wouldn't waste so much potato, but I hated potato peelers. They were way slow, and messy too. So, I sneaked the paring knife from the kitchen drawer because, the way I saw it, how a person peeled potatoes had little bearing on the way one lived one's life.

I sat on the back porch, pail at my feet, wooden bowl for potatoes next to me, singing Little Jimmy Dickens songs and peeling. The potato sack weighed a thousand pounds, but nobody cared that I had to drag it from the kitchen to the porch by myself. If they didn't care about me, I wouldn't care about them. They weren't like me anyway. They couldn't understand things even when I explained it to them, like where was the end of the sky. It had to be there, and one of these days I'd find it and go. Granny told Mama she ought to take me to a doctor because I might be touched, but I didn't know what that meant. She was peculiar anyway, so I didn't spend a whole lot of time worrying about her. She found my poems one day and said I was crazy, so I knew she couldn't understand much.

It took forever to peel those potatoes, but I did it. I didn't want any for supper, though. They disgusted me by that time. From a ridiculous game to peeling the things was enough for one day, thank you very much.

Granny's voice suddenly screeched through the house. Sounded like the pigs out back when Grandpapa swilled them.

"Jessie Mae! I told you to peel them taters with the peeler. How come you done peeled 'em with the knife"?

"I didn't. I used the peeler like you said to do." I smiled. I knew it looked nice because I practiced it in the mirror.

"You're lying; you, critter!" She was furious.

Knowing the fly swatter was coming next, I ran into the living room where Grandpapa and Daddy smoked and talked about the weather and the crops. "Grandpapa! Granny's trying to swat me for nothing. She's just lying; I didn't do nothing."

When Daddy saw the long belt of peeling in Granny's hand and the tiny potatoes she was throwing at me, he knew who had lied. He did not like it when people lied, and I did it a lot because I couldn't figure a way out of things by being honest. This lie was one too many, though. A spanking was coming, and I knew it.

For the first time in my life, I surrendered. But I decided to mull it over in bed later, and work out something to get even.

Painted Nails

After supper on Saturday nights,

9 liked to sit on Mama's bed and watch her put on makeup and paint her fingernails before she went out dancing with Daddy. I knew they'd come home fighting, but it was special to watch her get ready, anyhow. As I watched, she would smile at my constant stream of questions.

We could hear Daddy singing in the bathroom while he shaved. Why would I think that something dreadful was about to happen? I could usually feel deep down inside if something bad was around the corner. That night, though, I had no clue.

I was so happy it felt as if I might throw up, which is what often happened in those days if I got too happy. I tried not to be too happy because of that. Being sick was awful, and getting unhappy again was just around the corner, so it made no sense to get up in the first place. Being with Mama, though, I could not help but be happy.

My legs didn't reach the floor and smashed out sideways on the bed, which made them look even fatter than they were, reinforcing my belief that I was the ugliest girl alive, especially when comparing myself to my mama. Why I had to look like Daddy instead of her was beyond my imagination. I was born looking like him. If I had looked like

Mama instead, I could have had all the boyfriends I wanted, and Maggie Bolton wouldn't have ended up with all of them.

"How come God makes some people look bad when they wanna look good?"

Mama glanced in the mirror at me, cocked her dark head to one side, hair bouncing as she did. Her hair was beautiful. Huge curls reached down to fondle her white shoulders. When I saw myself in the mirror next to her, it scared me. My hair was so thin my ears stuck through. It was straight and flat, not curled or bouncy like hers. Even when I shook my head, my hair didn't do anything but lay there.

"You don't make any sense sometimes, Jessie, Why did you ask that?"

I shrugged. "I don't know. Just thinking about it, I guess. How come God didn't make me look like you? I didn't need to look like Daddy, did I?"

She poked at her hair, fluffing it more. "I don't know. Guess you just have to stop thinking about it and make the best of what you got."

The grand finale came. I was so excited I thought my heart would jump right out and land on the floor next to the bed. Mama was painting her fingernails bright red, like the women in the movies who wore feather scarves that drug the floor behind them.

Mama's nails were long and sharp. When she felt that I needed dealing with, she would dig them into my skinny arm until I winced. She knew well how to stop me from running through the kitchen while she cooked. That was to grab a pinch of skin between her nails and twist. I still sometimes have nightmares about that. When I looked at my stubby, peeling nails, I sagged. No matter how hard I tried not to bite them, I always did it, so they never grew. Mama forever fussed at me, "Don't bite your nails," but even when I managed to leave them alone, they wouldn't grow. They were too soft and bendable, and I'd get them caught on the sheets or the wash towel, rip them off, and bleed.

When she finished painting her nails that night, they were beautiful. Daddy would have to be the proudest man at the honky-tonk. How could he help but love such a vibrant person as my mama, even if she did frown and push her glasses up when she was unhappy. She was still the most beautiful woman in town, except maybe for the high school Quarterback's mother who sat in the stands and smoked cigarettes. She looked like a heavenly angel to me. I made a promise to myself that I would smoke like her someday.

"Mama, don't you thank Daddy's gonna be happy you look so good tonight?" I smiled at her, thinking she would smile back, but she didn't.

"Your daddy's never happy about a thing I do." She acted, all of a sudden as if she were angry, but I could not understand what I had said to cause the change in her.

By the time that they were ready to leave, I was on the settee pouting because I had to do what Darcy told me to do while they were gone. That was depressing. The only good part of Saturday nights was watching Mama get beautiful. The rest of it was horrible.

Darcy bossed Bobby and me around, making us wash the floor behind the settee repeatedly, even though it was already clean. We had to clean other things that weren't dirty, too. She was a bossy sister, and mean. It wasn't fair that she could be mean to me, and I could not be mean to Bobby. He was Mama's pet, though, and I guess that was what made the difference. Darcy said we had to keep the house clean in case Daddy shot Mama and people came to pay respects. It didn't matter to me; if they didn't like it, they could clean it up themselves. But Darcy was the boss when Mama and Daddy weren't there, so I had no say-so in the matter.

During the week, Mama's fingernails got little white specks on them. She called them chips. By the end of the week, they were no longer pretty. I knew, though, that they would get better on Saturday night. She let me paint my nails once, but the next day they had specks and didn't shine at all. I cried because it was terrible seeing them look like that so soon after I had painted them.

I wondered what it was about being a mama that made your nails ugly and speckled, deciding that it must be best to go dancing if you wanted to be pretty. If you didn't care how good you looked, you could be a mama and have specks on your nails. Either way, pretty or plain, I loved Mama. She was the only thing that mattered in my world. Even when she pinched me and twisted, I loved her. I didn't like it one bit when Daddy was mean to her. She was so beautiful when she two-stepped with him in the living room that it took my breath away. They were a handsome couple, somebody said.

Daddy let me stand on his toes and two-step with him sometimes. I was toe dancing with him one night when I decided I had rather dance and be pretty than ugly with children that loved me. That way, I could have long red fingernails but no children to pinch with them. It didn't seem that life was too fair most of the time. Mama had both. She was pretty, and she had children that loved her. I'd have to be content with one or the other because I knew that I didn't want specks on my fingernails.

Darcy put us to bed before Mama and Daddy came home, but I had not gone to sleep because I couldn't sleep well with Mama gone. Saturday nights made me nervous. They didn't usually come home happy, and their yelling made me feel like throwing up. I thought I would do just as well staying awake. That way, I wouldn't be startled awake, which was worse than staying awake. I could tell if they were fighting, by the sound of the car turning into the driveway.

This night the car came into the drive crooked; I heard it do it. Mama got out quickly, yelling that Daddy wasn't any kind of a husband or he'd buy her some rings like Betty Faye's, and she'd have a Cadillac to drive instead of some rattletrap Ford. There was going to be big trouble. I covered my face with the sheet, but I couldn't breathe, so I uncovered and prayed I wouldn't see blood.

Daddy followed her into the house. I heard a slap, so I figured he'd hit her. I wanted to cry, but jumped out of bed and crouched against the wall instead. I pulled my legs up to my chin and held them there, rocking back and forth. It always seemed to help. Someday, I would get out of this place and find a place that had a man who was kind to people. I wasn't sure this family was even related to me, so I wouldn't miss them much. Mama screamed, and the backdoor slammed so I knew she'd run outside and I sure wasn't going to stay in that house with her gone, so I knocked the screen out of the window and climbed out, whispering her name.

"Mama. Mama. Where are you?" I waited, in case she moved.

I soon made out a figure hopping around, trying to hide and I followed it. It was Mama, bleeding from the nose and trying to find the foxhole that we had dug to have hickory nut wars with the kids down the road. I grabbed her hand. It was trembling like mine. I pulled her to the hole. Just as we reached it, Daddy yelled he was going to kill us all and started shooting the twenty-two in our direction. Mama pushed me in the hole and jumped in just as a bullet whizzed by. It parted her hair down the middle instead of on the side where she generally kept it parted. I started to scream, but she put her hand over my mouth and said he would hear us and we'd be buried in this foxhole.

We heard rustling and held our breaths. Soon, we made out two figures and knew that Darcy and Bobby were trying to find us. I sure was glad we dug that hole. They jumped in with us, Darcy whining Daddy was a crazy man and somebody ought to put him out of his misery. Bobby was crying we were all going to die, and he didn't know if he would go to Heaven or the other place, so he needed to talk to a preacher before he died. Mama tried to calm us down. I was fed up with the whole thing and with all of them.

I thought about waiting until Daddy fell asleep, then getting that gun he liked to scare us with and shooting him. If I did, the rest of them could at least have some peace, and I didn't care anymore about living in jail with bad people. But when Daddy wasn't drinking, he was a regular daddy, and we loved him. Mama said it was whiskey talking when he acted like this. I started to tell her my plans when she took those fingernails and pinched the dickens out of my leg.

"Ouch! What'd you do that for?"

Another pinch. "Don't you ever let me hear you talking like that again, Jessie Mae. Talking about killing your own daddy. You ought to be ashamed."

I could not believe my ears. The man was trying to kill her and her children, and she was pinching me and saying such a thing. How was I to understand such people? They made no sense at all. I decided to keep quiet and mind my own business for the rest of the night. In the morning, when he was sleeping, we could get in the house and pretend we were regular people for a while. I leaned against the side of the foxhole and closed my eyes.

The morning was like every other day. Daddy snored while Mama cooked and coffee perked as if nothing bad had ever happened. We headed for the smell of food, knowing everything would be okay for a while. Mama seemed happy after these bouts. Who's to know what makes people tick? I put my arms around her waist from behind, and she turned the sizzling bacon, ignoring me.

"You smell good, Mama."

She pulled my hands from around her because she wasn't the touchy type, but I knew it wasn't because she didn't love me. When she did, I saw her fingernails, and it scared me to pieces. They had white specks all over them.

"What happened to your fingernails? They got white spots everywhere. How'd they get that way so quick? They were pretty last night."

She looked at her hands and shrugged. "Guess it must have been that foxhole and all that dirt."

"Dirt makes your fingernails get specks on 'em?"

I thought only doing mama things like washing and cooking and pinching kids did it. Here I was, learning plain old dirt could do it. I didn't like hearing such a thing. Dirt digging was my favorite pastime. Hunting for worms and pulling them apart to watch them wiggle in opposite directions to become two worms was something I loved to do. They reminded me of prissy church women.

Mama nodded. "Dirt's the worst thing there is for fingernails." She put the bacon and the toast on the table. I climbed into my chair next to Darcy.

"Well," I thought, "I don't really want long, red fingernails if I can't play in the dirt." The thought made me feel better for some reason. "I can have children if I don't have to have red fingernails at the same time." I smiled to myself.

Funny how God can make bad things turn out to be good things in the end. I could be a mama with lots of children, and I could cook and wash clothes and pinch my kids. And I could play in the dirt for the rest of my life.

That's when I knew that I didn't need to have long, red fingernails. I was going to be like the woman on television who had the kind husband that didn't get drunk or two-step, and I was going to have children I could pinch with stubby nails.

I bet that woman played in the dirt when she was a little girl. Wonder if she pulled worms apart.

Pick it up Darcy

I didn't like to rob the eggs

from under Grandma's chickens.

Darcy generally did it. The chicken coop was dark and scared me, and the chickens didn't like for me to do it, so whatever the chickens wanted, the chickens got. Since Darcy was bigger than I was, she felt obliged to boss me and, one day, decided to teach me how to get the eggs, against my fervent wishes.

Daddy said the best way a person could get over being scared was to just do it, so Darcy drug me to the coop and forced me in. She said, so that I could get used to being in there. Every time she shoved me in, I'd run back out, and she'd push me back in until, finally, she gave up.

"Oh, forget it, stupid. You can't do it cause you ain't smart enough like I am."

I knew that wasn't it; I just didn't want to do it. That was different from being stupid. It made me angry when Darcy said it, though, so I snatched the egg bucket and ran. Darcy chased after me, yelling she would kill me if she caught me. Little and wiry, I could climb quickly, so slinging the handle over my shoulder, I gripped the chicken coop wire and before she could grab me I was on the top, grinning and making faces at her and sing-songing.

"Ninner, ninner, ninner! You can't get me."

She threatened until she was blue in the face but could not get me down. All of a sudden, she turned around and walked away, leaving me perched on top of the coop. My heart flopped over. Not sure if she'd tattle or not, but sure that I could not get down before others came out and saw me, I was beginning to panic about being up so high when she returned, dragging a ladder she had found in Papa's shed.

"I'll get you down, you brat. You can't get away from me, and when I get you I'm gonna beat your butt, you hear me?"

I heard all right. I stuck my tongue out at Darcy and stretched my mouth to make it uglier. She deserved it, bossy thing.

"I'll tell Mama if you hurt me, Darcy. I will."

"Go ahead; tell her, tattle tell. I don't care. I'm gonna make you sorry for living."

The ladder banged against the edge of the coop, and Darcy climbed it like a monkey, fuming and fussing as she did. I pedaled against the rooftop with my heels, trying to get higher so she couldn't reach me. She kept coming. Darcy had always been stubborn as a mule, Daddy said. She would do it or die if somebody dared her. I had never been much that way. Putting that much effort into anything wasn't pleasant for me. I didn't want to be beaten to a pulp this day, though, and she would do what she said she would do, and I knew it. My heart started fluttering and beating hard. I could hear it in my ears. That meant that I was doomed.

"Got you!" She screeched at me as one hand grabbed an ankle and yanked, pulling me, sliding on my bottom, toward her and the roof's edge. I was a goner and knew it. That's what Daddy called people who had lost at something: a goner. I had never been able to win over Darcy. I spent hours on end planning how to smother her while she slept, or stick my foot out and make her fall down the front steps, but I never could get up the nerve to do either one.

Darcy made me harmonize with her when she'd sing her country songs to show her great talent. Bobby was too little, and Mama and Daddy couldn't be made to do anything they didn't want to do, so she chose me. She would force me to sit on the pile of boards Daddy kept stacked behind the house and stare at her mouth.

"Follow me. Let's hominy. You watch my mouth, and if you mess up, I'll beat the tar outta you with one of Daddy's two by fours. Now sing!"

I followed every word as if glued to her mouth, scared to death my hominy would be wrong. I was afraid to make a mistake for fear she'd kill me, but after those years, I never wanted to sing again.

I kicked at her with my free foot. "Let me go, Darcy! I'll tell. Let go."

She started that high-pitched giggle of hers and pulled herself onto the roof using my skinny ankle. For a minute, I thought she was going to pull my leg off. Then she was on the roof with me. Scared she would push me off, I started screaming, contorting my face as gruesome as I could, yelling louder every time I had to stop and take a breath.

"Shut up, Jessie. Shut up. Mama's gonna hear if you don't be quiet."

She clamped her hand over my mouth the way she did when she'd try to smother me. I kicked harder, trying to escape her grasp, and one hard kick landed on the ladder. Darcy screamed.

The ladder began a slow descent from the coop, stood straight in the air, then headed away from us. Darcy released my ankle to try and catch it but was too late. It was absolutely beautiful. It moved in slow motion like a ballerina, ghostly and soft and floating. Suddenly, though, it flew backward like a bird and hit the ground with a loud crash, like a million pots and pans in a quiet kitchen. We covered our ears with our hands.

The quiet was deafening. Not even the chickens squawked. We leaned over the edge and stared at the ladder in front of the door to the chicken coop. Darcy looked at me. I looked back at her, figuring how to protect myself.

"Pick it up, Darcy. You dood it."

Papa heard the crash and came running. When he saw us on top of the coop and the ladder on the ground, he grinned, hands on his hips. We smiled at him.

"Hey, Papa. What you doing?" Darcy's voice was squeaky sounding. She sighed and looked around like she had planned to be trapped up high like that. I was terrified and showed it.

"Well, now, what we got here? You two happy up there?" Papa kept grinning at us, sitting up there like two trapped birds.

All of a sudden, fear took control of me. Until Papa had come out, I hadn't thought much about it, but now I was terrified to be this high up.

"I want down, Papa. Get me down."

"You want down, you say?" He stayed put.

I nodded, swallowed. "Yeah. I want down now. Get my daddy. Get him right now."

He just stood there. Fear grew into a panic, and I cried louder until I was screaming. With my screams came more kicking, the way I did when I was "coming apart" as Mama called it whenever I got that way. Papa knew me, too, and he knew that if he didn't stop picking at us and get me down, I would end up throwing myself off out of pure terror.

"Hold on, Jessie. Be quiet. I'll get your daddy, and he'll get you down. Be still, now. Hang on to her tight, Darcy. Don't let her jump."

He left us and came back with Daddy, who took care of problems like this in a calm, quiet way that always stopped my attacks. He held his hand up as if to tell me to stay there and be silent, then picked up the ladder. He leaned it against the coop, climbed up to me and pulled me toward him by my leg. I had to sit on the ladder and bump down on my behind because I was trembling too hard to do it any other way.

Once on the ground, my legs buckled when I tried to stand. Darcy skimmed down with no problem. She was afraid of nothing, which made no sense at all to me. The world was a dangerous place for children. Mama said it was. Things were every place to grab and eat you alive if one wasn't careful. Darcy didn't seem to care, though, and acted as if nothing could harm her. Sometimes, I wished I was more like her and not such a scaredy cat. I admired her even though I was afraid of her and sometimes thought I hated her. She was strong. I liked that in people.

I never climbed on top of the chicken coop again, and Darcy quit trying to force me to get the eggs from under the chickens. She knew I hated those creatures and acted as if she finally understood and respected my feelings. I still didn't trust her completely but decided I'd at least give her the benefit of the doubt. Daddy said we should always give people that even if they didn't deserve it. For now, I would do that much for her.

Bobby had to start helping with getting the eggs. He would do it even though he didn't want to because he was an obedient child. He never questioned an order, just did what he was told to do, even if it made him cry. I hated that in him. It made people like him more than they did me, and being liked was important to me. I felt I had that right and didn't like him taking away my rights.

Darcy and Bobby gathered eggs for Grandma to cook for breakfast. I would sit on the screened porch and feel guilty. Until then, I had never felt there was one reason I should feel guilty about anything, so it confused me. Guilt had never been a part of my life. Watching them laughing together, hearing their chatter inside the coop, made me feel both guilty and jealous. Grandma was the one we told our problems to, so one day, I crept into the kitchen where she was.

"Grandma? Can I talk to you?"

She blessed me with her twinkling eyes. "You sure can, Jessie." She stopped cooking, sat down at the big kitchen table and pulled me to her. "What is it, honey?"

When Grandma's knotted fingers touched my arm, it felt as if she had pulled a quilt over me. My chin quivered.

"Grandma, I did something wrong, and I don't know why I did it."

She smiled, crinkling her face into the look I loved. "What could you ever do that's so wrong, Jessie?"

I swallowed. "Well, I told a lie about Darcy." I gazed at her, my chin in the air to say I had a right to do it, but it made me sad.

She raised her little black eyebrows, waiting for me to continue.

"I said Darcy pushed the ladder off the chicken coop, but she didn't. I did. I kicked it when she was trying to get me. She didn't push it down."

Grandma smiled and pulled me closer to her soft, plump breast, squeezing me just enough with her arms. She rocked me side to side, saying nothing. Finally, she held me at arm's length and gazed into my eyes.

"Jessie, you're getting to be a lovely young lady. Telling the truth is part of coming of age. Now, what do you think you ought to do about this?"

I twisted my lips and sighed, then looked into her kind, understanding eyes. Grandma never made me feel that I was bad, even when I was. "Well, tell Daddy I did it and Darcy I'm sorry?"

She nodded and hugged me. "Now, dear, you go and get your sister and brother for breakfast." Her eyes told me what I had to do.

I skipped to the chicken coop and heard Darcy and Bobby inside gathering more eggs and laughing. All of a sudden, Bobby started laughing, but Darcie screamed. I ran inside to find them both hopping up and down, yelling at the top of their lungs, broken eggs everywhere, and a chicken lying still and quiet on the ground.

"What's wrong? What's wrong, ya'll?"

Bobby hid behind me, dirty hands grabbing at my clothes.

"Stop it, Bobby! Let go. What ya'll yelling about?"

"Jessie, Darcy kilt a chicken! She kilt a chicken!"

Darcy stared at Bobby, then at me, her mouth open, eyes wider than I had ever seen them. Tears began to fill those black eyes and her chin quivered. I had never seen her look that way. She was usually so strong and bossy that she couldn't cry. But here she was, almost there.

Suddenly, she clamped her mouth shut, wiped her eyes, stood very straight and stalked toward the house, the empty egg pail in her hands. We followed hand in hand. When she got to the kitchen, she set the bucket on the table and faced Grandma. She took a deep breath,

"Grandma, I killed a chicken and broke all the eggs. I'm sorry. I don't need no breakfast." With that, she turned around and walked out of the house.

I followed her, staying far enough behind so she wouldn't know I was there. She walked into the pasture so nobody could see or hear her, and when she got to the big oak, she sat down next to it. Leaning against the oak, she pulled her knees up to her chin and laid her head on her knobby knees. I could see her shoulders shaking, and I could hear her sobbing. I watched until she finished crying, wiped her eyes, got up and brushed off her dress. Then she walked back to the house. No one would ever know she felt bad at all.

Bobby followed Darcy around trying to tell jokes and play tricks, but she ignored him. She didn't seem angry with him, just treated him like a little brother. That's when I began to understand Darcy, even like her some.

I couldn't sleep that night for watching Darcy's face as she slept beside me. She looked so sweet when she was asleep. I thought about her bossiness and how we felt she was so mean to us. Then I remembered Mama and Daddy and their fighting. I thought about how Darcy would grab Bobby and me and shove us under a bed or in a closet and tell us to be quiet. Sometimes, she'd take us outside and hide us in the bushes. We thought she was mean to us. But now I knew. She was a little girl who had a great big job. Taking care of Bobby and me. I cried that night, for Darcy.

The next morning, everybody gathered around Grandma's big table to eat. Grandma hadn't mentioned the loss of yesterday's eggs. She just had more oatmeal than usual, and her eyes sparkled at Darcy just as much as they did for us. I couldn't stand it any longer.

"Ya'll, I gotta say something."

All eyes turned my way, waiting. The noise of utensils clinking stopped so that it was quiet. I swallowed. This was a hard thing I was about to do because I had never been too honest.

"Darcy didn't push the ladder down. I kicked it down."

The eyes kept staring. Nobody said a word.

I looked at Darcy. Her head was bent over like she was praying. Then I saw one big tear slide down her face.

Bobby jumped up as if he were confronted with a firing squad. "And she didn't kill no chicken, neither. I did.

And I broke the eggs. I thought it was fun till Darcy started screaming."

Both of us sat down, hands in our laps, waiting for our punishment. It seemed forever before anyone spoke. It was Grandma.

"Children, you're both growing up real good. I appreciate you telling the truth. Darcy, I need to ask you to forgive me for not seeing the truth. I know you, child. I ought to know you would never do nothing like that."

Darcy kept her head bowed. "That's all right, Grandma." Her voice sounded little.

"I'm really sorry, Darcy. You're the best sister in the world." As I spoke, I stood to go to her. In the process, my knee caught the tablecloth and jerked it, pulling several plates right off the table onto the floor. Food spilled everywhere. Aunts, uncles, and cousins sat staring at the food on the floor, forks still in their hands.

I thought I would start bawling right there in front of everybody. Until Darcy's head popped up.

"Pick it up, Jessie. You dood it."

Promising Heddum

Nothing terrified me more than the threat of someone telling Heddum I had been bad. I lived in fear of the old black man who ate disobedient children. On this day, though, I was not worried. Even when Mama told me not to get my clothes grimy, I obeyed, so when we headed to town I had no fear.

Mama was a slow driver. When she drove, it was easy for Bobby and me to stick our heads out the window and let the wind blow in our eyes until they were so dry it was hard to close them. Daddy drove too fast for us to do that without the wind stinging our faces. We had to be careful which way we faced when we spit out the window if he was driving, too.

We drove along, Mama now and then taking her hands off the steering wheel to push her glasses up, and swerving when she did. The wind was weak and warm, perfect for poking heads out of windows. Spit drooled at the corners of our mouths. It was a perfect day.

Mama drove around the Courthouse square several times before finding a parking spot. I was fine until I saw Heddum, dragging his sack filled with who knows what.

"We can't park here, Mama."

She shrugged and maneuvered the car into the parking space.

I tapped her on the shoulder, pointing at him. "Heddum's here."

"I don't care if he's here; he's got to be somewhere."

"But you can't park here, Mama."

"Jessie, shush!"

"Mama! You can't park here!"

I fell back against the seat in horror, flinging the back of my hand onto my forehead like the woman who swooned in the movie Daddy took us to see. Bobby's eyes grew big, and his face turned ashy, but he didn't say a word. Darcy didn't care where we parked. She was the oldest and could go in the stores with Mama while we waited in the car.

"I can't believe you'd leave your own children where Heddum can get 'em. You know he eats children!"

"Jessie, for goodness sake; hush!" Mama shoved at her glasses.

I glared at her, using the meanest look I could muster, but she ignored me and got out of the car, stuck her head back in the window, and hissed at me.

"Jessie Mae, stay here and watch Bobby. Don't let him get out of the car, and don't you get out, either. You hear me?"

I whispered. "What if Heddum tries to get us?"

"He won't."

"But, what if he does? Just pretend."

"Then, I'll miss you."

With that hateful remark hanging in mid-air, my own mama strolled away. I watched through the back window, fear swelling up like somebody choking me to death, knowing Mama did not even care if Heddum got her own children. Darcy made faces at us. Bobby looked petrified. Generally, I hated him, but this day felt sorry for him. And for myself.

"Bobby, stay real still. Maybe he won't see us."

I rolled the windows up but soon, we were sweating profusely, and I was worried we would not be able to breathe much longer. Tears filled Bobby's blue eyes, so I put my face close to his and whispered, "Don't you dare make any noise. We can't let him hear us. Okay?" He nodded, but I knew he was beginning to disintegrate before my eyes, and I didn't know what to do to help him.

I wondered what kind of mother would leave her children to be eaten. Ever since I could remember, I had heard about the large black man who carried a cane whittled to a point to stick in paper and stuff it in the sacks. He collected cans and glass, and children, too, they said, taking them to his shack to cook and eat. The men in Mundy's store said he ate cans and glass. I don't know how he managed to swallow glass without cutting his insides.

Heddum inched closer, and we slid lower until I was flat on my back in the seat.

"I fank I'm gonna frow up." Bobby's face looked pale and strange.

"Don't you throw up! He will eat you." He moaned softly, but it seemed as if his moaning echoed off the Courthouse walls.

I had a feeling he was near before I saw him. His breathing made the car move, and nobody else could possibly breathe that hard. I stretched my neck to see where he was and came face to face with the whites of his eyes. I screamed. Bobby cried. The car shook from little feet kicking against the seats in terror.

Heddum grinned. I heard a calm voice and stopped screaming. Holding on to Bobby, I looked at the old man and tried to look fierce.

"Get away; you, carnival!" I pointed a trembling finger and tried to sound like Daddy when he was angry, but he didn't move away from the car.

"Get away, man!" Bobby wanted to seem strong, too, but it came out like a kitten trying to meow with a dog hanging on its throat.

Heddum spoke. "Hey, ya'll. What you doing in that hot car? You afraid I gonna hurt you?"

We nodded in unison. He smiled. "I ain't never hurt no chillun."

I sat up and pointed a wagging finger, the way Mama often did at me. "Oh, yeah? Well, how come people say you do?"

He stopped smiling and scratched his head. It surprised me to see that he was sad. His big shoulders slumped. "I don't know why they say that. It ain't right. I like chillun."

Somehow, I knew he was telling the truth. He wasn't planning on eating us. But, if he didn't eat children, why did our mama and daddy say he would?" Something was wrong with this picture. I felt sorry for him. Also, it was too hot to hide. Since he had found us, anyhow, I figured there was no reason for us to stay shut up in the heat. Mama warned us not to get out of the car. She didn't say we couldn't open the door to get fresh air. I opened the car door.

"You want to come in and rest your feet?"

He shook his head. "No'm, best keep on working."

"What work you do?" I sat on the seat resting my feet on the running board. Bobby hung over my shoulder, trembling and breathing in my ear.

"I pick up trash and sells it over to the dump."

"They pay you for trash?"

"Yes'm. Well, the people ain't paying me for trash, just paying me for picking it up and making the Courthouse square nice and clean."

"Well, that's good, I guess."

He nodded and wiped sweat from his forehead with his arm.

"You eat cans and glass?"

"No'm, they just say I do. Don't know why people say that." His look hurt my heart.

"If you don't eat cans and glass, then you must not eat children?" I laughed. My hands had almost stopped trembling.

"I ain't never ate no chillun. That's a bad thing people say."

As quick as a rabbit, I jumped out of the car and wrapped my arms around his big waist. "I'm sorry people tell fibs about you. It don't feel good when people do that." Bobby put his arms around me from behind as if he were hugging us both.

"Jessie! Bobby! Get away from him!" Mama was screeching. It scared me so bad, I jumped, knocking Bobby backward onto the running board.

"Mama, Heddum's sweet. He don't eat children."

She shushed me and slung me into the car by my skinny arm, threatened Heddum, and drove away. I looked back and waved. He waved and punched the point of his stick in the paper on the ground. We drove in silence. Bobby and I were not hanging our heads out the windows.

Heddum was nice. All my life, they had threatened to call him if I didn't mind, so he could eat me, they said. Now it looked like they had been lying to me all along.

On the way home, I asked, "Mama, how come nobody likes Heddum?"

"What?"

Her voice was so shrill I decided to wait until later to discuss it. Darcy called me a nincompoop and stuck her tongue out. I stuck mine out at her, crossed my arms, sat back, and fixed my mind on serious thinking.

At supper, I waited for what I felt was the proper time to talk about Heddum and the lying all around. "Daddy, how come ya'll don't like Heddum?"

"Because. Eat your supper."

"That ain't a good reason, Daddy. He ain't done nothing wrong. He's just selling trash."

Daddy's neck turned red; he dropped his fork and glared at me. "Watch your tongue, young lady."

I knew I should be quiet and not say another thing, but it seemed that Heddum was nothing like they said he was. "He's nice. He don't eat children or nothing. Not even cans and glass. I wanna know why ya'll say he does. Cause that ain't right."

"I said because, and that's good enough for you."

"No, it ain't. If what you say ain't the truth, then you've been lying, and you told me lying was bad." I had pushed him far enough and knew it.

He shoved back from the table, grabbed me by the arm and marched me to my bedroom. There, he removed his belt. My heart crawled up to my throat when I heard a knock at the front door. I hoped that by the time company left, Daddy might forget about spanking me.

"Ma'am." I heard Heddum's voice and my heart pounded so hard I thought it might leap out and flop all over the floor. I followed Daddy to the front door.

Mama slapped her hand over her mouth, and her glasses slipped down her nose. When Daddy got to the door, he found himself face to face with Heddum.

"What in the hell? Get off my porch! You wanna see me, you get to the back door." He slammed the door in Heddum's face.

"Daddy, you're mean. He's a nice man."

"He ain't coming in my front door, by God!" I had never seen my daddy so angry. His face was purple, and he was breathing hard.

Heddum made his way to the back door, waited for Daddy to quit yelling, and then spoke.

"Sir, I ain't come to make no trouble. I just wanna say I ain't hurt no chillun. People say I do, but I don't. I just try and earn a living, sir, and I treat ladies and chillun with respect. Ain't caused nobody no trouble."

Daddy glared at him and slammed the door. "Jessie Mae, get your tail in here."

I got a spanking for being the cause of a black man coming to the door and speaking that way to a white man: dreadful thing to do, apparently. I thought it was a good thing. White or black, it made no difference to me. It seemed to me that Heddum was the better man of the two.

From then on, whenever we went to town, Mama wouldn't let us stay in the car. We had to go to the stores with her and Darcy, and stand around waiting.

One day, I saw Heddum outside, dragging his sack. Making sure Mama wasn't looking, I scooted out the door hollering, "Hey, Heddum!" He didn't look up, just kept ambling along, shoulders stooped.

"Heddum! It's me, Jessie! How you been doing?"

He didn't answer, and it devastated me. He was ignoring me. That was not proper. Mama had taught me to speak when someone talked to me. Doing that was fitting. I decided there was no reason to be pleasant any longer since he evidently didn't know how to be polite. It was either that, or he did not like me, and I didn't want to think about that.

Mama was searching through the store for me when I got back. "I've been looking all over for you. Where've you been?"

"I saw Heddum, and I wanted to tell him hey." I was proud of my honesty.

"That was a nice thing to do."

Her remark surprised me. I thought she would tell me how disobedient I was that she was going to tell Heddum and he would eat me. The eating thing, though, was down the drain by now and wouldn't work anymore.

"Jessie, it was wrong to tell you that Heddum would eat you and do mean things to you. I don't know why we said that. I guess he was somebody to blame stuff on to keep you in line, and he wouldn't do anything back. I don't know. I'm sorry. Will you forgive me?"

I threw my arms around her. "I'm glad you don't hate Heddum, Mama. He's real nice. Can I go ask him to come for supper?"

"My heavens, no! I didn't mean he could be our friend. I just meant that what we did was wrong. He's still different from us."

"No, he's not, Mama. He's a man like Daddy and Sam and Uncle J.W. It ain't fair. Just because he's got a dark tan don't mean he's not like them."

"Hush up, now! Come on; let's go home. I guess your daddy's gonna have to deal with you. You'll understand how things are one day."

I ate that night in silence. I had thought my parents cared about people. None of it made sense to me.

Several weeks later, Aunt Emma visited Mama, and I played on the porch with my dolls, eavesdropping in case they said something about me. Aunt Emma tried to whisper so I wouldn't hear, but I did.

"Did you hear? That old Heddum up and died. They found him in the Courthouse square sitting on the bench.

Some say he died because he was sad, but I don't know why in the world he would be sad. Seems to me he had an easy life, what with no job or nothing to worry about. Tell you the truth he'd been acting funny all year, you ask me."

I wanted to die myself right then. Sweet, gentle Heddum never knew how much I loved him. I was angry with everybody and decided that, from now on, I would like anybody I wanted to like, and Mama and Daddy would not have a thing to say about it. Nobody could say anything about it. I wouldn't even let people know, and wouldn't ask for anybody's opinion or approval.

The next day, Mama went shopping at Mary's Boutique, and I slipped over to the black funeral home. Nobody was there except the man who laid people out, and he pointed me to where they had laid Heddum.

As I stood over his wooden coffin, I touched his sweet face and cried. Bobby sidled up beside me and put his hand on my arm.

"Heddum," I whispered. "I'm so sorry you were sad when you died. I wish I had told you how much I loved you. Maybe I can come to Heaven and tell you in person someday."

We visited Heddum until the emotions ended. Before we left, I promised him that I would never lie to children to make them fear anybody. Just because they were different. Different was a good thing.

Rabbit Gravy
Just Ain't for Me

Growing up, eating rabbit wasn't anything much different than eating venison, which at the time I didn't know was Bambi for, if I had, I simply would not have eaten it, whipping or not. I never was one for obeying when the order disturbed my psyche so much I couldn't go to sleep because my mind kept rehashing the thing all night. Didn't seem worth it to me. I'd just take the spanking and go to bed without supper. Suited me fine.

I ate rabbit because I'd never thought about it. Daddy and Bobby always did the hunting and Mama fixed it for us to eat, so I figured it was food and meant to be eaten. That is until Daddy decided it was time for Darcy, Bobby, and me to learn how to skin a rabbit.

That night felt funny even before it began, and I never did like times like that because they reminded me of the night our house burned down. That same feeling hung around me and all around the house, so I knew something was coming that I was not going to like at all. But not knowing for sure what it was, I had to go on about my business pretending everything was like any other night. Then I heard Bobby crying and Darcy screaming.

Darcy always shrieked when she saw things she didn't like to see, but Bobby wouldn't usually cry about that, so I went running to the kitchen. Mama was in there humming, the way she did when something bad was going on, but she didn't want to think about it. Daddy was outside the back door with Bobby and Darcy, and he was cussing. I didn't want to stick my head out there, but I always seemed to do what I didn't want to do, so I stuck it out. I wished I hadn't done that.

Darcy had a dead rabbit by the back legs, and her face was bright red, and all scrunched up like she was smelling something awful, and Bobby was standing beside her crying, "I fank I'm gonna frow up, Daddy." Daddy just kept cussing and telling Darcy to hold that damn rabbit still and yelling at Bobby that he was going to be next if he didn't shut up that cry babying. I guess I should have sneaked back to my bedroom, but being inquisitive by nature, I didn't.

"Hey, ya'll; what you doing?"

I smiled because somebody said I looked good when I smiled and it looked to me like they needed me to look good so they'd feel better.

Daddy jerked his head at me, motioning for me to come out there with them. I shook my head no.

"That's all right, Daddy. I think I'll just stay here." I smiled again, this time a little nervously.

"Get your tail out here, Jessie. It's time you learned how to skin a rabbit, too."

I could not believe my ears!

"I ain't gonna skin no rabbit!"

He glared at me with a look that said I was going to skin that rabbit or he was going to skin me.

"What'd you say to me?"

I looked at Darcy again with her scrunched up face and repeated what I'd said. Who did he think he was, anyhow, telling me to do something like that to one of God's creatures! He stepped toward me, leaving Darcy standing there holding that half-skinned rabbit.

"Jessie Mae, I told you to get your tail out here, and I mean what I say."

He looked down at me with the look he'd give Mama sometimes when she didn't mind him, but I didn't care. There was one thing I was not going to do, and that was to hurt a poor little animal that hadn't done anything but be alive when Daddy found him.

"No! I ain't gonna do it, and you can't make me. You can kill me, but I ain't gonna hurt nothing like that."

I stuck my chin up as high as I possibly could without stretching my neck too tight and stared into Daddy's eyes. I could tell right away he knew I meant what I was saying and was trying to figure out what to do to make me mind to "save face" as he always said. I was really scared, though, because I just knew I'd die right then and there if he forced me to hold that rabbit. I saw a movie once where some people skinned this man, and I had never forgotten it, so I knew what was going on.

I whirled on one foot and took off running through the kitchen, the living room, and out on the front porch, Daddy chasing behind me. Mama started screaming for him to let me go because I wouldn't listen anyhow and he'd just have a heart attack getting so upset. Darcy was still standing there with her eyes closed holding that poor rabbit, but Bobby ran toward the shed where Daddy milked the cow he kept in the backyard. Bobby had a hiding place in that shed, and we never had been able to find it. He was tiny so he could fit into small places.

I was about to jump off the porch when Daddy threw up his hands at me and turned around. He'd given up trying to catch me, and he probably knew he couldn't make me hold the rabbit anyhow. If he put it in my hands, I'd just drop it. I would not clutch that dead rabbit. I kind of felt sorry for

Darcy for having to keep holding it while Daddy finished skinning it, but Darcy bossed me around so much, half of me sort of felt good about it, too. Bobby just stayed in the shed, or wherever he was, for the rest of the night.

I didn't sleep too well that night for dreaming about people skinning people and rabbits skinning people, and me running in circles screaming for somebody to help.

The next day was kind of quiet, the way it usually was when one of us had gotten the best of Daddy. Mama said he was pouting, but it looked to me like he was mad because he'd lost. I felt pretty good about it myself. Until supper.

Darcy and I set the table for Mama while she got the food ready for us to eat. It smelled wonderful, and my stomach was almost cramping I was so hungry. We could never eat between meals. Mama said we wouldn't eat our supper if we did, so all of us were always hungry and grabbed the food and stuck it in our mouths as soon as we could.

This night, however, when I sat down between Daddy and Darcy, my eyes landed on the plate in the center of the table. It looked tasty and smelled great, but something inside me didn't want to look at it.

"Mama, what's on that plate?"

I looked across the table at Mama, and she tried to act normal without looking into my eyes.

"Jessie, for goodness sake! It's just the meat for supper. Give me your plate."

She still wouldn't look at me.

"I ain't too hungry for meat, thank you anyway."

I tried to smile but my mouth felt like it wanted to go crooked, so I swallowed and reached for the potatoes and gravy. Nobody said anything while I poured the sweet gravy on my potatoes and biscuit. I could hardly wait until I put a big bite in my mouth.

Suddenly, Darcy burst out laughing. Then, everybody started guffawing and were all looking at me.

"What's wrong with ya'll?"

My stomach felt uneasy, and I knew something was up that might get to me.

Darcy could hardly wait to tell me, either.

"You just poured rabbit gravy all over your potatoes."

I looked at the white, creamy sauce in front of me.

"It ain't rabbit."

I looked at Mama. She looked down at her plate.

"Mama, it ain't rabbit, is it?"

If she didn't answer me, I knew I would panic and start screaming. "Mama?"

"Jessie, it doesn't matter if it is. Eat your supper."

I shoved my chair back and pushed the plate toward Mama. No way was I going to eat anything that poor rabbit had been cooked in. I wanted to run until I could run no more. How people could be so mean to things was beyond my way of thinking.

As I ran from the kitchen to my room, I barely heard Daddy's voice, but every word stuck in my mind like briars in a blackberry patch stick to your legs.

"Jessie, you gonna have to starve cause everything's alive and if you eat it, you gotta kill it."

I never ate rabbit again, and no one could force me to eat a deer or a chicken or a cow. We experienced a terrible drought several years back, and an article in the paper told about scientists who had equipment that could hear corn screaming as it died from lack of water. I remembered what my daddy had said: that everything was alive and if I wanted to eat it, I had to kill it. I thought about that for a while and came to this compromise conclusion.

I decided to eat only those things that did not scream loud enough for me to hear and look at me with eyes like my own. So, rabbit gravy ain't for me, but corn fritters just might do.

Saving Whiskey

"Jessie, get out of that truck this minute;

do you hear me, young lady?"

Mama slammed the screen door and stomped across the kitchen. It never failed but that she caught me doing something I wasn't supposed to do. I sighed and shut the truck door. She would appreciate it if she knew what I was doing in Daddy's truck.

Mama didn't like it when he hid whiskey under the seat in the pickup, so when he would finally pass out, she would sneak it out and pour it down the sink. That aggravated Daddy, and he'd take his rage out on all of us. I figured if I got his whiskey and poured it out, he wouldn't get mad at Mama and take it out on us. Mama didn't think things through, though. She jumped to conclusions, usually wrong ones, and rarely gave me a chance to explain. I knew I had to be the only one in this family with any brains at all.

"I told you she'd hear you. You're so dumb, Jessie. How come you don't listen to nobody?"

"Oh, shut up, Bobby. You just shut your trap. It ain't no business of yours anyway. I can do what I want. I want to do this. You just do what I say and make sure she don't catch me again."

Bobby shrugged his skinny shoulders and stuck his head out so he could peek around the truck to watch the kitchen door, in case she came out again. He was supposed to warn me if she did so I could get out before I got in trouble. It was critical that I do this if I didn't want Mama to find whiskey and do something stupid.

Regardless how many times Daddy came home and jerked the tablecloth off the table, dishes and all, Mama never knew when to be quiet. Darcy would end up hanging on to Daddy's arm, trying to keep him from hitting Mama and calling her a horse. We told her he'd be nice and buy her candy and cute dresses if she'd just let him be when he had a red face and smelled like whiskey. But, no, she would not listen to us kids.

Every time, she would tell him how useless he was and how she was going to take us and leave him forever, so he'd get mad. I never could figure out why she didn't know that kind of fussing wouldn't work. Her high-pitched whining even bothered us. It had to bother him worse. I liked it when Daddy bought presents for us. He was happy and a lot of fun when he was like that. The other days he acted tired and seemed in a bad mood when he came home, so he would eat supper and sit in his recliner reading the paper, not saying a word to anybody. We would have to be quiet so not to upset him and make him yell at us.

I opened the truck door as quiet as a mouse and made a space big enough to squeeze through, letting the door rest on its hinges so it wouldn't make any noise. Bobby stared at the house as if he were in a trance, now and then rubbing his eyes with his fists. I felt under the seat and came up with a greasy wrench and some cigarette wrappings.

I crawled across the seat. Nothing. There was no whiskey so tonight might be dull, but at least I didn't have to worry about fighting. I slithered through the opening, slid to the ground, and pushed the door shut. When I turned around, I stood nose-to-nose with Mama. She was scowling, and her glasses were slipping down her nose without her bothering to push them up. I closed my eyes, hunched my shoulders to my chin, and waited.

"Jessie Mae, I told you to get out of that truck! What am I gonna do with you? I oughta tell your daddy what you been doing. He'd straighten you out, by golly."

She grabbed my wrist, dug her fingernails into the skin, and pulled me across the yard. My heart was pounding so hard I could hardly hear her yelling, so I knew I was going to die right there. I was in for it; I knew it, and I deserved it. I wasn't mad at Mama, but I was furious with Bobby. How did he let her sneak past him? When I looked back, I knew how. He was still sitting there, curly blond head peeking around the truck, eyes bigger than I'd ever seen them. He would never figure out how she got past him and I wasn't going to explain it to him, either. Let him think he was dumb. He was anyhow.

Dragging me behind her, Mama broke a switch on her way in. Once inside, the usual hopping around went on as the switch slapped and stung my legs. Switching was the worst kind of punishment as far as I was concerned. The only worse penalty was when she'd make me get my own switch and bring it to her. If I got one too little, or too limber, she'd send me back for a meaner one.

I had to set the table for supper, and my stinging legs had thin red lines all over them. Every time I took a step I thought about having to get in the tub to bathe. I could feel it sting just thinking about it. I sniffed and put the plates down, sniffed and set utensils on next to the plates, until Mama had had enough and told me to quit sniffling because I sounded like a pig.

Daddy was home on time so we knew he'd smell normal and not be red, but he would be in a bad mood. Darcy liked to talk at the table and fuss at Bobby and me, so this should be a bad night, all in all, I decided.

"Daddy, I need some money for a dress to wear to the Glee Club dance Friday night."

Darcy smirked at him, her nose in the air, thick red hair fluffed all over her head and face and shoulders, full lips pursed as if this was the most important thing Daddy could ever imagine. I held my breath because I knew the supper table was not the place to demand anything of Daddy.

Mama stood at the end of the table with the biscuit pan in her hands, and her trusty dishrag slung over her shoulder. Her eyes didn't move from the pan to Daddy. Bobby and I sat as still as we could. I thought he'd never break the silence.

"Ain't got it, Darcy. I'll get it after supper."

He kept eating, and I felt faint. A lady from the old South who lived in a columned house and carried a fan and wore an enormous hat that hid her eyes would have fainted. But, since I was Jessie of this house, I decided to react normally.

"That ain't fair! You let Darcy have anything she wants and don't let me have nothing."

"Go to your room, Jessie Mae. I don't need no sass like that from you."

He did not even have the decency to look me in the

eye, just kept on smacking at his food. Mama cast her sad look at me, but I didn't think she had any right to be pleasant to me after what she'd done. Darcy sneered and tossed her curls, so I stuck my tongue out to let her know I disapproved of her. I pushed my chair back and left the table, Bobby's squeaky voice trailing behind me.

"Jessie's bad . . . Jessie's bad."

The rest of them smiled at him as if he were funny, so he kept taunting as I trounced down the hall. I had slammed the bedroom door before I gave it thought, then turned around to catch it, too late, and heard Daddy coming down the hall. I glanced at the window but couldn't think fast enough. By the time that he'd finished thrashing me with my own hairbrush I was hurting all over and mad at everybody in the house. Just because I wanted to protect people from Daddy's outbursts. Nobody understood me or even cared about my feelings at all. They didn't deserve me. I promised myself I'd leave there one day, and they'd be sorry they treated me the way they did.

I talked to the mirror, pretending it was Jonathan, and I was the beautiful woman he loved. It was a famous love story I had heard about somewhere. This man gave up his throne to marry a lady who was a common one and even divorced, but I wasn't sure what that was or whether to really believe the stuff I heard around this house. I liked me and got along well with myself, so sending me to my room was not the worst thing they could do to me.

"I'd rather be here with me than there with them anyway," I thought. I proceeded to enjoy playing with my doll, making believe and forgetting all that had happened.

After supper, Daddy left to get Darcy's money but he stayed way too long, and we started to get edgy, the way we did when he'd been gone long enough that we knew how he'd look when he came in. Sure enough, his face was red when he got home, and he smelled like whiskey. I looked at Mama and panicked. She had on her frown, and her glasses were sliding on her flaring nose. I tried to think of something to tell her to get her mind off of him, but no matter what I said, she had her mind made up. She was getting angrier with every word he said. I didn't like him much, either, but I knew if she'd be quiet he'd sit down and fall asleep. Then we'd all be fine.

She didn't keep quiet, though. Another night of battle before he finally fell asleep and we could come out of our hiding places and get in bed. We slipped in quiet like mice, our clothes still on in case we had to jump up and run again.

My eyes burned from lack of sleep at school the next day, and I came close to falling asleep on my desk, but the teacher yelled at me. Bad day, bad night.

Home from school, Daddy's truck eyeballed me, inviting me to visit. I didn't care if she switched me or not; I was going to get that dreadful whiskey and pour it out. It made our lives miserable, and it didn't deserve to live. I opened the door and hopped in, no attempt to be quiet. The whiskey was under the driver's seat, and I pulled it out. Even half-empty it smelled like Daddy. I gritted my teeth.

"Know what, whiskey? You're a dead duck."

I lifted the bottle and slammed it on the dashboard. Smelly liquid flew everywhere: the truck, the windows, the seats, me.

"Oh, goodness!"

I looked at the broken bottle. I couldn't believe I'd actually done it. Daddy was going to kill me for sure this time. I had to figure out a good excuse, but I was so horrified I couldn't make my mind reason with itself.. Then, I knew what to do. I was so proud of my resourcefulness I could hardly stand it. I would lie. Nobody knew I was in the truck, so I'd just lie about it. He wouldn't know. He might even think he did it. I laid the broken bottle on the seat and sneaked out of the truck, into the house, and dried myself off. I was brilliant. Enthralled with my creativity.

Daddy didn't feel well at supper and ate without talking. Darcy prattled on about her plans for the dance and Bobby made up songs that irritated me to no end. Mama gazed at me, a sweet expression in her eyes. When I would look at her, she would smile. Darcy had something planned, but I was afraid to ask for fear it might be something I didn't want to hear. I couldn't tell if she was happy with me or planning to fix me, as Daddy said when he planned revenge on somebody for some reason or other. I ate silently; praying no one would know what I'd done.

"Jessie, honey, I like that perfume you've got on." Mama's voice was soft and tender hearted.

I started to say I didn't have no perfume, how would a ten-year-old girl get perfume in this house, then decided I had best keep quiet. She knew what I had done. I almost choked trying to get the cabbage down. Daddy eventually left the table, and I could breathe a little easier.

Mama smiled, "Jessie, I'm sorry I fussed at you about getting in the truck. I know what you were trying to do now, and I appreciate it."

When she took her plate to the kitchen, I followed. I

wrapped my arms around her waist from behind, and she patted my hands. I loved my mama so much. All my plans were built around trying to keep her safe and happy.

"I'm sorry, too, Mama. I want you to stay safe."

She nodded, "I know, hon. It's all right."

Later, Daddy went to the truck to get cigarettes from the glove compartment and stayed a long time. We waited in silence, wondering how angry he would be when he came in. Suddenly I realized something.

"Hey, ya'll! Daddy can't say nothing about the whiskey. He ain't supposed to have it, to begin with."

We watched him when he came in and picked up the newspaper. Whether he figured out what actually happened or not, he never said. But I never found another bottle of whiskey in that pick-up truck.

The Rite of Stockings

Daddy didn't like to visit Mama's family because he liked his family best. At least that's what Mama said. So, once a year we drove to Dahlonega to spend a day or two with her mama and daddy. I loved Grandpapa but tobacco dribbled down the sides of Granny's mouth, and she said things like how big Darcy's chest was getting. I avoided her as much as possible.

Grandpapa was a big, gentle bear of a man. When he lifted me, it felt as if I might fly to Heaven. I felt safe around him and loved it when I heard his voice. If I could have spent my life with him, I would have. When we visited, cousins came over to play with us and sometimes we shot at the garbage cans with B.B. guns. I was a good shot, too, because Daddy had taught me how to shoot by holding a kitchen match in his mouth and telling me to light it without shooting him. He said we'd better not miss, so we never did.

Grandpapa took me to the front porch one day to let me eat pecans and watermelon while he sat in the rocker and talked. He cut moon-shaped slices of melon with his pocketknife, and I ate until I could eat no more and my hands were sore from cracking nuts against each other.

Nothing was better than listening to Grandpapa. He often told me a beautiful love story of five brothers from

England, or somewhere over the ocean, who all married Indian girls. He said that was why I had black hair and high cheekbones; I had Indian blood running through my veins. Grandpapa said I was beautiful and I believed him because he never lied. At least I'd never known him to. It was later that I found out the five brothers and Indian girls story was not exactly real.

Hand in hand we would walk across the road to the store for candy, Grandpapa whistling like he always did. I never heard him do that at home. Instead, he was quiet and kept to himself. It seemed to me that Granny yelled at him about everything, so I figured he didn't have a mind to whistle because there was no real reason for it. I loved going to the store with him because it made him happy. I also liked Mrs. Johnson, the woman behind the cash register. She had long red hair and green eyes, and she blinked them a lot. I wondered if she had an eye problem but never asked. She paid little attention to me, anyhow, just talked to Grandpapa.

He would greet her, then sit down beside the potbellied stove and talk about fishing and Mr. Martin's lost cow, and how the space people must have stolen her. While he chatted with the other men, I'd make myself at home checking out the candy jars. As fast as Grandpapa could buy it, I could eat it. Those days were divine, until suppertime.

Grandpapa never wore a watch, but he always knew when it was time for supper. He'd stand up, stretch, and call my name. Hand in hand we'd stroll back across the road to the old two-story house that needed some paint. My heart always jumped when I heard Granny's screechy voice.

"Jessie, it's time for supper. Get your hands washed. Peggy, get the rest of them younguns in here. It's time to eat."

Granny would wipe her greasy hands on her stained apron and stomp back to the kitchen. I didn't like to be around her, but did like the warm biscuits she kept on top of the wood stove and wanted to put sugar in them while they were hot. The smell of coffee filled the kitchen because Granny kept a pot warming on the stove all day. The men liked to have hot coffee when they came in, and the women poured a cup when they sat down to rest their feet.

"I feel awful, Mama," I whined. My stomach cramped. Mama put the back of her hand to my forehead.

"You feel warm. You been eating something you ought not to?" She frowned at me; the kind that said she was worried. I felt good when Mama frowned like that at me. It meant she cared about me. Sometimes she made milk toast for me when I was sick, and that night she knew milk toast was the last thing I needed.

I lied about the pecans, watermelon, and candy. "No, ma'am. I had breakfast and dinner; that's all." I felt guilty about not being honest, but I didn't want to get Grandpapa in trouble. He told me I probably shouldn't tell he bought the candy for me, but he didn't say anything about pecans and watermelon.

"Oh, I forgot," pretending to remember, "I eat a couple of pecans and a slice of watermelon, but that's all."

Mama smiled and led me to the kitchen where the smell of food did me in. I took off for the back porch and barely made it to the steps before I threw up. It was horrible. I had never felt so sick and thought I would never finish being sick. When it was over, my stomach was sore, and after I'd washed up, Mama put me to bed.

"Mama?"

She leaned over me. "What you want, Jessie?"

"I'm sorry I lied to you." My chin quivered. I had no idea why I was honest, or why the lie had bothered me, but also knew that I must tell the truth. "I eat a lot of stuff."

She smoothed my hair. "I know you did."

"You do? How do you know?"

"Well, you got to remember your Grandpapa's my daddy. He raised me, and he's the same now as he was when I was a little girl. He's always bought candy for people he loves, and he gets them pecans and watermelon, too."

"How come you didn't say nothing when I lied?"

She sighed. "Your Granny don't like for your Grandpapa to go over to the store where Mrs. Johnson is."

"Mrs. Johnson's pleasant, ain't she Mama?"

She laughed. "She might be, but my mama don't like her at all."

"How come she don't like her?"

"I think it's got something to do with your Grandpapa buying Mrs. Johnson stockings for her legs and none for Granny."

"How come he buys Mrs. Johnson stockings; don't she have none?"

Mama had a laugh that I loved but rarely heard because she was always sad about things my daddy did. Her laugh tinkled like a tiny bell.

"Mama, does Grandpapa love Mrs. Johnson and not Granny?"

"I don't know," she shrugged. "It's just always been this way since I can remember, and Granny don't like to know he's been visiting with her. So, it's our secret, okay?

I promised I would never tell Granny. I might not like to be around her, but I wouldn't make her unhappy on purpose. After all, she was my mama's mama, and without my mother, I wouldn't even be here. Thinking about it like that, I wanted Grandpapa to love Granny and not Mrs. Johnson. It didn't seem right for him to like some other woman better than he did his own wife. Maybe I should talk to him about it. I decided that I would do just that. I would speak to him about it in the morning if I felt good enough to do it.

Every time I'd start to drop off to sleep my stomach would hurt, and I'd have to run outside, so it was a long night. I was afraid to move when I woke up for fear it would start again. The smell of sausage and coffee felt wonderful drifting through the house and settling on my nose, and I was hungry. I put on my robe and scurried to the kitchen. Daddy and Grandpapa were sitting at the table eating silently. Mama was helping Granny finish breakfast for everybody.

Nobody sat down together at Granny's house, the way we did at home.

"Howdy, girl," Granny slapped me on the back before I could move out of her way. "Feeling better this morning?"

"Yes'm. I feel a lot better. I thank I can eat some food."

I climbed over the bench on the backside of the table and watched Grandpapa mix the butter in molasses, stir it with his fork, and then sop it up with a hot biscuit. I wanted to eat molasses and butter that way, but it made me sick to my stomach thinking about it, so today was not the day to try. Mama set a bowl of oatmeal and a glass of milk in front of me, and I was glad. It felt soft and smooth even before I put it in my mouth. She knew not to put anything greasy on my plate.

Every time Grandpapa and I slopped the hogs together, there was one missing. I hated making friends with the pigs because every time I did, it would disappear. I knew what was happening and didn't like it. I watched the fork take sausage to Grandpapa's mouth and thought to myself, "cannibal."

"Grandpapa, I need to talk to you." It came out of my mouth without my planning.

"Oh, you do, do you? What you need to talk about?"

"I need to talk by ourselves. It's private, and I don't want nobody to hear us." I felt important making that statement. I'd heard people make it on television and it sounded wise.

Grandpapa scraped his chair back. "Okay, let's go to the porch, ain't nobody out there." I followed his stooped form to the back porch, which was built around a well. When we needed water, we'd pull a bucket up and drink from a wooden dipper hanging on the side of the bucket. I dreamed of having a house like that someday. At home, we had to go outside and pump water into a bucket and bring it inside. That was harder than this.

"Grandpapa, I'm a little bit worried about you."

"Oh?" His eyes twinkled, and the corner of his mouth turned up some.

"Yeah, I am. I've been thinking about Mrs. Johnson."

"Mrs. Johnson, huh? What about her?"

"I was wondering how come you like her better than Granny."

"What makes you think I like her better than your Granny?"

"Because you buy her stockings and don't buy Granny none. She probably needs some, and if she don't need 'em, she probably wants some."

"How come you think your Granny might want some stockings?"

"I just figured. Maybe that's why Granny fusses at you all the time."

He smiled and leaned the wooden chair back on two legs. "Your Granny just likes to whine, Jessie."

"I don't think so, Grandpapa. I think it hurts her feelings because you don't like her good as you like Mrs. Johnson."

"Where'd you get so much sense, Jessie Mae?"

I shrugged. "I don't know; just born with it I guess."

Grandpapa told me how he met Granny. He said her hair was black like a bird and straight as a board, and hung to a waist so tiny he could reach around it with one hand. He could probably pick her up with one little finger, and he loved her so much it made his heart hurt. I don't know why they started fussing. He said he never figured it out. She wanted him to be something he wasn't, he said, but I didn't know how a person could be something they weren't.

We heard Granny fretting about nobody ever helping her with the dishes, so we went back inside the house.

"Granny, I'll help with the dishes." I held my head high in pride that I was quick at being good.

The deep voice I loved so much spoke. "Jessie, you go your way now. I'll help your granny."

It surprised me to hear him say that, but I think it surprised her more. She stood in front of him like a tiny rabbit caught in a trap, and he took the iron skillet from her little hands. I decided to mind him. He most likely wanted to be alone with her. As I left, I heard his low voice rumble. "You're too dainty to be holding such a big pan."

"What's done got into you, you red-faced Injun?" She screeched, and I held my ears.

I shook my head. Didn't she know that kind of talk was hard? His answer, though, was soft.

"I never thought you would want stockings. Guess I was wrong. Been buying them things for the wrong woman. You think that's right?"

I didn't hear her answer, so I don't know what she said or what he said after that. But I didn't have to listen to any more fussing. The kitchen was quiet except for the clatter of dishes.

After everybody was asleep except me, I heard Grandpapa telling Granny that it was gonna be all right. The next morning, she was smiling. I had never seen her happy in the mornings before. Grandpapa went to the store alone, and she didn't even get mad. He didn't stay long, though, and when he came back, he had a pair of stockings.

Winkie

"Mama! Something's wrong with Winkie!

He's got yellow stuff coming out his nose."

9 pressed my face to the screen door and watched Mama

slide an iron skillet full of cornbread batter into the oven. She wiped her hands and turned toward the door. "He's probably just got a cold, Jessie; he'll be all right."

For the most part, Mama kept me calm, but I didn't feel calm this day. Winkie was important to me, and I didn't want him to be sick. My puppy made me happy, and it was important for little girls and their pets to be happy. Every time I had a dog or cat something awful happened to it. If it didn't run away or get killed by a car, or another animal, my daddy took it off and came back without it.

"How come he's got stuff coming out his nose then?"

My own nose was squashed against the screen, grimy hands cupped around my eyes.

"I don't know. Sometimes dogs just get runny noses; that's all."

She paid no more attention to me. I sat on the cracked cement steps that led to the back door and thought about why I never got complete answers to my questions. It seemed to me that grownups had no idea what I was talking about whenever I asked them questions. They just said I'd find out someday. Well, for Heaven's sake, anybody would know that, even a kid! I never wanted to wait, though, and needed an answer when I asked a question. I decided they didn't know the answer but didn't want to look bad in front of kids. After all, grownups were supposed to know everything and when they didn't know something, I guess it embarrassed them.

Mama said that supper would be ready soon, for me to call my brother and wash up so we could eat. I grumbled, but in the end, did what she said. It wasn't sensible at my house to disobey our mother. She'd tell our daddy, and there'd be misery to pay. I never knew for sure what he'd do to me, except for the time he told me not to go to Shirley's house after school and I went anyway. It wasn't long before Shirley's mother said my daddy was waiting out front for me. When he got me home, he whipped me with my own hairbrush and sent me to my room without supper. It taught me a good lesson, I suppose. I never went to anyone's house again without permission.

"Bobby! Time for supper! Come on in and wash up Mama said."

Bobby took his own good time strolling to the house like he always did. On the way, though, he paused at the dog house and peeked inside. Suddenly, he whirled wide-eyed and took off toward the house yelling, "Winkie done died, ya'll."

I flew to the dog house, ignoring Mama's instructions completely. When I got there, my heart was wobbling almost out of my chest. Winkie was on his side struggling to breathe and wheezing. His nose was white, and his eyes rolled backward into his head. He was so small and helpless. I knew the world had best just stop right there and somebody help my puppy or nobody would ever be forgiven.

"Bobby, get Mama! We gotta do something quick. Winkie's dying!"

Bobby ran, which I sure was glad about; otherwise, he'd never make it in time to save Winkie.

Mama rushed out the door with the dish rag in her hands. I don't remember ever seeing her without a dish cloth in her hands or over her shoulder. I'm sure I must have, but I can't remember it. Daddy stayed in the house to finish reading the paper. I squatted in front of the doghouse with my head and the top part of my body inside, petting Winkie and calling his name.

"Get out of the way, Jessie. Let me see him."

I tilted my head to let Mama see how bad off he was. By now I was desperate. Peculiar whimpering noises escaped my body all by themselves. Mama patted my back.

"Get him out of the dog house, hon."

That scared me. When my mama called me "hon" it meant that there was something to be worried about.

Mama ran into the house for a towel and then wrapped Winkie in it so we could take him to the doctor. She turned off the cornbread, and we loaded him into the Chevrolet and headed toward town about five miles down the road. Daddy stayed home.

We lived in a small town. The veterinarian had been dead for a long time, but his wife kept the business going, even though she wasn't a real vet. She'd learned how to tend animals by helping her husband all those years and everybody accepted her. She always had a passel of animals all over the place barking and yapping and howling. The lady was small and old but pleasant, so I didn't mind too much when I handed Winkie over to her. It seemed like she liked him. She smiled at my little blonde puppy packaged up in a blue-striped bath towel.

"Let me see what we got here."

She headed for a cramped, odd smelling, silver-colored room, Winkie in her arms. The room had a metal table smack in the middle, and she laid him on it. I couldn't decide what the odor was but knew it couldn't be dead dogs like Bobby said it was. I'd smelled dead rats before, and it wasn't that same smell.

The lady unwrapped the towel. Winkie's ribs stuck way out. He struggled to breathe. It didn't sound like a dog when he's breathing the right way. I wanted to cry, but I didn't. Mama had told me before we left the house not to be a crybaby and make her sorry she brought me with her.

Darcy stayed with Daddy so she could set the table and turn the cornbread back on when she thought we'd had enough time to get to town, talk to the doctor, and get back. Mama always planned things out. If she didn't, Daddy didn't like it, and he'd sometimes go off and come back and jerk the tablecloth off the table with the dishes still on it. It wasn't enjoyable when he did that, and none of us liked that kind of shock. We didn't like to help Mama clean food and dishes off the floor either, so we tried hard to keep Daddy happy.

The doctor said that Winkie had the 'stemper. I didn't know what that was, but Mama said it was a cold, only worse. They both said he'd no doubt get well soon, but he had to stay with the lady until he was better because she had to give him medicine. I could visit him every day after school, though.

Mama said she didn't know how on God's green

earth she could get me there; she didn't have a car during the day since Daddy drove it to work, except on grocery day, and that was only one day a week. I said I could walk to the doctor's house after school until Winkie got well. I could walk the five miles home, too, no problem. Mama didn't like it much, but she had a sweet heart and understood that I needed to visit my puppy so she said it would be all right, she supposed.

My teacher, Mrs. Betterly, just so happened to be going that way every day and dropped me off at the doctor's house so I could spend some time with my puppy.

Mr. Morton passed the doctor's house every day at just the time I had to leave. He'd take me home because he said, "I don't live too far from you folks; don't mind a 'tall."

I never did have to walk.

Visiting Winkie was sorrowful. He knew me when he saw me or heard me and tried to wag his little tail, but it would kind of flop on the towel he lay on. His eyes couldn't stay open by themselves, either, so I had to hold the skin off of them so we could look at each other and I could tell him how much I loved him. He said he loved me, too, in his own way.

One day the doctor had him strapped to a board and

turned upside down so the stuff in his lungs that made him 'stemper could drain out his nose. He looked terrible and didn't even try to wag his tail when I told him that I loved him and needed him to get well. I cried that night, but nobody heard me with my pillow over my head.

I got to the doctor's house one day, and she met me at the door crying and shaking her head. I knew why but didn't like it one little bit and said no real loud and stomped into Winkie's silver room. He was on his side on a soft blue pad. I couldn't hear him breathing. When I put my hand on his side, it felt hard.

I wanted to scream and throw things around the room like Daddy did when he was drunk, but I stood real still like a soldier, hoping the awful feelings would stay inside and not come out and frighten the other animals. They didn't feel well, either. I knew the doctor tried to save Winkie and wasn't angry with her. I just couldn't decide how to stay alive myself right then. Anger grew like a monster inside of me, but I didn't know what to do with it so it would go away from me.

Nobody said anything about Winkie at supper that night until Darcy said he was precious and she really did like him; she just pretended that she didn't. I said it didn't matter; he was dead now and she couldn't make it up to me even if she tried for the rest of her hateful life. Nothing mattered to me. I went to bed after supper and didn't even bicker with Darcy or Bobby, either one. Mama and Daddy were even nice to each other that night, and that made me madder for some reason. I thought "How come people want to be kind to you when awful things happen? How come they can't be like that when things are okay?"

Black Beauty, Winkie's mother, seemed downhearted for a few days like maybe she knew her little boy was dead, even though she never did get to see how handsome he was. I think she knew, though. I heard somewhere that mamas have an extra sense and that makes them recognize their children even if they never get to see them. Daddy said Black Beauty was a Cocker Spaniard. To me, she was just an old black dog with long ears and no eyes. Sometimes I wondered if she understood us when we talked because, being Spanish, she might not understand English. I loved her but loved her son more.

When I thought about Winkie, I could smell him. He had the sweetest puppy smell in the world.

I felt like his death was my fault; he was my responsibility; Daddy said he was. I should have taken care of him but couldn't figure out what it was that I did or didn't do to make him sick. Mama said it wasn't my fault. She said puppies just got the 'stemper sometimes and nothing could stop it or be done to cure it. I still felt to blame.

After Winkie had died, I slept with my stuffed animals and pretended they were real. At least they couldn't suffer and die like real pets did. Every time something died, I got more afraid of death myself. It came so quick, and nobody could do anything to keep it away. Then, when it took hold, it made things hard as a rock. That scared me half to death.

My grandpapa was hard like that when I sneaked into the living room and touched him when he was in his casket. It scared me so bad I almost died myself, right then and there, but I was more afraid of turning stiff than of dying, so I kept on living

I couldn't sleep very well for a long time on account of dreaming about Winkie, but in my dreams, he didn't have the 'stemper. In them, he ran and jumped, his huge ears flopping in the air, and his pink tongue dangling from his sweet mouth. I decided not to think about him dead and hard. Instead, I would remember him sniffing courageously, scampering and daring because that made me not so sad.

I came home from school one day, and Daddy was home from work. It scared me a little bit because he never did stay home, even when he was sick or hung over. I nervously opened the door. Mama wasn't yelling so I figured Daddy wasn't drunk or mad at her.

When I walked in, they turned around, both of them grinning at me like they knew a secret that I didn't know. I waited. Something strange was up. I could feel it in the air. Daddy stooped down in front of me so we'd be eye to eye.

"Jessie, I been searching the paper for something ever since that dog of yours up and died. Finally found it."

He grinned. I shrugged. I didn't understand, but he acted as if I should.

Mama had her hands behind her back, and she was grinning too. I thought they might be getting strange in their old age until I heard it. A whimper. Just a little one. My heart beat harder like it was trying to come out of my body.

Mama and Daddy burst out laughing like they'd done the finest thing ever in the whole wide world, and then my mama stuck a little black curly-haired dog in my face. I smelled his puppy smell first. It was just like Winkie's precious smell. And then I saw his big, brown eyes and felt his warm tongue kiss my face. My heart was so happy it felt like a giant balloon about to burst.

I looked at Mama; turned toward Daddy. He grinned. "I found him in the paper." He nodded over and over, so proud of himself.

I hugged his waist, then hugged Mama and the puppy together and then grabbed him from her. I stuffed my face into his soft fur. He squirmed and whined and licked until I was howling. Maybe it wasn't always wrong for Daddy to read the paper after all. Especially if he was searching for friends for his own children.

Paper Doll and I sit on the steps sometimes and talk to Winkie, just to let him know I still remember him. We're delighted together. Like I said earlier; it's important for little girls and their puppies to be happy.

Well, guess I'll go for now. Mama's cooking cornbread for supper and Daddy's reading the daily paper. Paper Doll and I like it when he does that.

Made in the USA
Columbia, SC
18 March 2021